THE RIDDLE OF THE SANDS

The Frisian Islands lie along the North Sea coast of Holland and Germany, and sailing around these islands can be dangerous, especially in bad weather, because of the sandbanks that lie hidden beneath the shallow waters at high tide. The channels between the sandbanks are narrow and easy to miss, and the sandbanks themselves change with the wind and the tides.

Arthur Davies is young, enthusiastic, and a brave and skilful sailor, who takes great delight in sailing his yacht *Dulcibella* through these difficult and dangerous waters. He asks his friend Carruthers to come out from London and join him for a sailing holiday, but his reasons for doing this only become clear to Carruthers after several days on board. It seems there is a riddle to solve, and a little mystery about a man called Dollmann. The two friends begin to investigate – and the commander of a German gunboat begins to take a close interest in them.

For the year is 1902, and sandbanks are not the only danger on this coast. The gathering storm-clouds of the First World War are slowly growing darker, year by year . . .

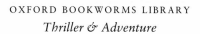

OXFORD BOOKWORMS LIBRARY
Thriller & Adventure

The Riddle of the Sands

Stage 5 (1800 headwords)

Series Editor: Jennifer Bassett
Founder Editor: Tricia Hedge
Activities Editors: Jennifer Bassett and Christine Lindop

ERSKINE CHILDERS

The Riddle of the Sands

Retold by
Peter Hawkins

OXFORD UNIVERSITY PRESS

OXFORD

UNIVERSITY PRESS

Great Clarendon Street, Oxford OX2 6DP

Oxford University Press is a department of the University of Oxford.
It furthers the University's objective of excellence in research, scholarship,
and education by publishing worldwide in

Oxford New York

Auckland Cape Town Dar es Salaam Hong Kong Karachi
Kuala Lumpur Madrid Melbourne Mexico City Nairobi
New Delhi Shanghai Taipei Toronto

With offices in

Argentina Austria Brazil Chile Czech Republic France Greece
Guatemala Hungary Italy Japan Poland Portugal Singapore
South Korea Switzerland Thailand Turkey Ukraine Vietnam

ISBN 978 0 19 479231 8

Printed in Hong Kong

ACKNOWLEDGEMENTS
Illustrations by: Paul Fisher Johnson
Maps by: Richard Ponsford

Word count (main text): 22,885 words

For more information on the Oxford Bookworms Library,
visit www.oup.com/bookworms

CONTENTS

PEOPLE IN THIS STORY

Carruthers, *who tells the story*

Davies, *his friend, and owner of the yacht* Dulcibella

Bartels, *Davies' friend, and captain of the* Johannes

Herr (Mr) Dollmann, *owner of the* Medusa

Fräulein (Miss) Clara Dollmann, *his daughter*

Frau (Mrs) Dollmann, *Dollmann's wife and Clara's
    stepmother*

Commander von Brüning, *a German naval officer,
    and captain of the gunboat* Blitz

Grimm, *captain of the* Kormoran

Böhme, *an engineer from Bremen*

THE REASON WHY

Why has this book been written?

In October 1902, my friend Carruthers came to my office, and told me the story of the yachting trip that he and his friend Mr Davies had recently taken in the Baltic and the North Sea.

The account of his adventures both astonished and alarmed me, and when he asked for my help in preparing this book for publication, I agreed readily. It is well known that Britain's coastal defences are dangerously weak, so the secret information discovered by Carruthers and Davies is of great importance, and I fully support their wish to make this information public.

The difficulty they had was that an Englishman, from an old and famous family, would be shown in their story to be a traitor, and this would cause pain and misery to an innocent young lady, whom they are anxious to protect. The names Carruthers and Davies, therefore, are not their real ones, and the names of all other persons in this account have also been changed.

But why publish secret information of national importance? Should it not be kept secret, known only to the government, whose job is to make good use of such information?

Indeed, that would normally be the best thing to do, but not in this case. The government, although informed of the great danger facing this country, has chosen to do nothing – and that is the reason why this book has been written.

London, 1903

1

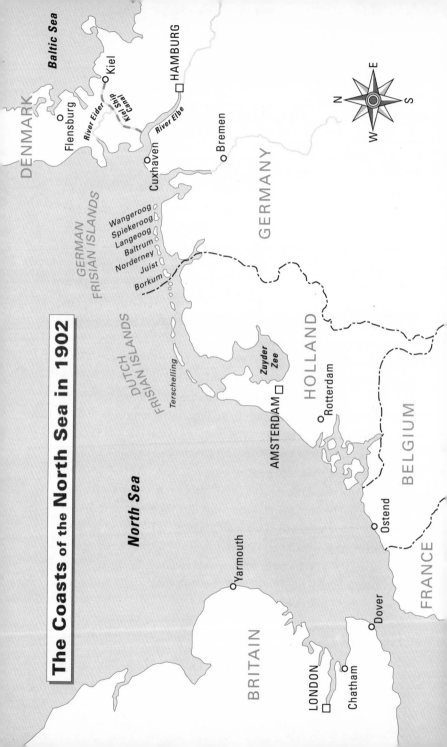

The Coasts of the North Sea in 1902

Baltic Sea

DENMARK

Kiel

Flensburg

River Eider

Kiel Ship Canal

River Elbe

HAMBURG

Bremen

Cuxhaven

GERMANY

GERMAN FRISIAN ISLANDS

Wangeroog
Spiekeroog
Langeoog
Baltrum
Norderney
Juist
Borkum

DUTCH FRISIAN ISLANDS

Terschelling

Zuyder Zee

AMSTERDAM

Rotterdam

HOLLAND

BELGIUM

Ostend

FRANCE

North Sea

Yarmouth

Dover

BRITAIN

LONDON

Chatham

N E S W

An invitation to the Baltic Sea

The letter arrived as I was dressing for dinner in my rooms in Pall Mall on the evening of 23rd September 1902. London was deserted at that time of the summer, and I had become very bored and depressed with my daily routine of work at the Foreign Office, and dinner at my club in the evening. All my friends were away enjoying themselves at country house parties, but here was I, a fashionable young man with a bright future, who knew all the best people and belonged to all the best clubs – and who was forced to remain in London because of my job.

I had encouraged my friends to believe that the Foreign Office could not manage without me during the summer, but the plain truth was that my work was neither interesting nor important. It consisted mostly of taking messages for absent officials, whose own holiday plans had upset mine.

Although my friends had sent me sympathetic letters, it was clear that I had not been greatly missed, and now, at the end of September, I realized another bitter truth. Two more days, and I would be free to start my holiday – but I had nowhere to go! The country house parties were all breaking up, and though I could always go home to Yorkshire, of course, which fashionable young man wants to spend his holiday with his own family?

I was, without doubt, extremely depressed.

So, when a letter, with a German stamp and marked 'urgent', arrived that evening, I felt a touch of interest, even excitement, as I opened it and read:

Yacht Dulcibella
Flensburg, 21st September

Dear Carruthers,

You will probably be surprised to hear from me, as it's a long time since we met. But I write in the hope that you might like to come out here and join me in a little sailing and, perhaps, duck shooting. This part of the Baltic is very beautiful and there should be plenty of ducks soon, if it gets cold enough. The friend who was with me has had to leave, and I really need someone else, as I'd like to stay out here for a while.

If you can come – and I do hope you can – send a telegram to the post office at Flensburg. I know you speak German perfectly, and that will be a great help.

Yours ever,
Arthur Davies

Then followed directions as to how to reach him, and a long list of various things for the yacht that he would like me to buy and bring out.

The letter was a turning point in my life, though I did not know it at the time. During my lonely dinner that evening I was undecided. Yachting in the Baltic in October! I must be mad even to think of it. I was used to the kind of yachting party that took place in warm summer weather, on comfortable, luxurious yachts with servants to bring meals and drinks. But what kind of yacht was the *Dulcibella*? Davies, I remembered, was not rich. We had been at Oxford University together and had been quite friendly, but I had not seen much of him in the three years since then. On the few occasions we had met, I found him rather dull.

His letter, too, seemed rather unpromising. His friend had left

4

him – why? The Baltic was beautiful – yes, but what about October storms? Did I really want to spend my holidays freezing in the Baltic, with a man who was sure to bore me to death?

⊕   ⊕   ⊕

Two days later I was on the night ferry to Holland, with a huge pile of luggage and a ticket for Flensburg in my pocket. I'd had to go all round London to find the things that Davies wanted for the yacht, and I felt I was being generous and unselfish. Davies had said that he needed a friend, so I was doing a friend's duty and answering his call. It was just possible, of course, that I might enjoy myself as well.

The train took me east, then north, through Germany, and by ten o'clock the next evening I was standing on the station platform at Flensburg, and Davies was greeting me.

'It's awfully good of you to come.'

'Not at all. It's very good of you to ask me.'

We watched each other cautiously. Davies, in ordinary old clothes, did not look like my idea of a yachtsman. Where were the fashionable white trousers and dark blue jacket, like the ones lying neatly in my big suitcase?

'You've brought a lot of things,' said Davies, looking anxiously at my luggage.

'You asked me to get most of them,' I replied. 'I've brought you the hammer, the rope and the rubber boots you wanted. Oh, and the gun you were having repaired.'

'Oh yes! Thank you. I didn't mean those. It's that large case. You couldn't manage with just the small bag?'

'No, of course not,' I answered, puzzled.

'Well, never mind. It's not far to the dinghy,' and he bent down to pick up my luggage.

5

'But where are your men?' I asked.

'Oh, I never have any paid men on the *Dulcibella*,' he said cheerfully. 'The whole fun is doing it yourself. It's quite a small yacht, you know.'

I looked at Davies in silent horror. Then I picked up my bag, frowning. 'Come on, then,' I said.

'You'll like the *Dulcibella*,' said Davies, a little anxiously. 'She's very comfortable.'

Loaded down with my luggage, we made our way in the dark towards the harbour. Davies stopped at the top of some steps that disappeared into the darkness.

'The dinghy's down there,' he said. 'You go down and I'll pass the things down to you.'

The stone steps were slippery, and I had only a wet piece of rope to hold on to. I went down carefully, conscious of collecting dirt on my trousers. Near the bottom, I slid on the mud and sat down with one foot in the water.

I climbed miserably into a very small boat.

'Are you ready?' called Davies from above. He passed down my large case, which almost filled the little boat. The rest of the luggage followed, making a big pile that shook dangerously every time I moved. Somehow Davies managed to climb into the boat, and started to row across the harbour.

'The yacht is a little way away,' he explained. 'I hate to be too near a town.' Then, a few minutes later, 'Look! There she is.'

In the dark, I could just see a small yacht with a light shining on its mast. Davies jumped on board, and tied up the dinghy. 'Now, pass the things up, and I'll take them,' he called.

I did as he said, thinking unhappily of the last time I had been on a yacht – the paint shining in the sun, the decks as white as

I went down carefully, conscious of collecting dirt on my trousers.

snow, the men eager to help. How different from this horrible, clumsy business in the dark!

When we had finished, I climbed on board. The deck was covered with boxes and cases. Davies, who was staring at my big suitcase, suddenly seemed to wake up. 'Come on!' he said cheerfully. 'I'll show you around.'

He dived down a ladder and I followed carefully. At the bottom I turned, and hit my head on the low ceiling.

'Mind your head,' cried Davies, too late.

I looked around, and saw, by the light of an oil lamp, that I was in a tiny cabin, almost filled with a large table. On each side there was a bench-like seat, above which was a shelf holding books, maps, and so on. Through a small door beyond the table I could see an old cooker. The whole place smelled of oil, cooking, and sea water.

'You see,' said Davies. 'There's plenty of room to sit up straight.' I wondered if this was meant to be a joke, as I was bent almost double. As I sat down, my knee came into contact with a sharp edge. 'Watch out for the centreboard,' said Davies. 'She's a flat-bottomed boat, you know, good for sailing in shallow water. And in deep water you lower the centreboard. That way we can go almost anywhere.'

He disappeared up the ladder and started passing down the boxes and cases. Soon they filled the small cabin to the ceiling. I heard him trying to push my case through the doorway at the top of the ladder.

'It's no good,' he said, reappearing in the cabin. 'You'd better unpack it on deck, and drop things on to your bed.'

He lit another oil lamp, and proudly showed me the other cabin, which had two narrow beds built along the sides. 'This is where we sleep,' he said. 'I'm not sure there's enough room for all your things, though. I don't suppose you could manage without some of them?'

'No, I couldn't,' I said crossly. 'Now, if you could move out of the way, I can get out too.'

He suddenly looked miserable at the way I spoke, but, tired and depressed, I pushed past him and climbed up on deck. In the dying moonlight I opened my case and took out some of the things. The rest – the clothes I'd worn on my last yachting holiday – I put back in the case, afraid that Davies might see them. I closed the case, and sat down on it. There was only one good thing about this depressing arrival – it wasn't raining. This thought made me look round at where we were.

The water was as smooth as glass. There was not a cloud in the sky, and the bright stars were reflected in the dark water – stars above and stars below. I could see a few little white houses on one shore, and the lights of Flensburg in the distance on the other. In between, the darkness hid the open sea. Everything was quiet except for Davies moving things about in the cabin.

How it happened I do not know, but suddenly my mood changed. Perhaps it was the miserable look I had last seen on his face. Perhaps it was one of those moments of clear-sightedness that people sometimes have, when I saw my silly selfishness compared with a simple, generous nature. Or perhaps it was the air of mystery about the whole trip. I suddenly felt ashamed of myself, a fashionable young man, tired and dirty, sitting on a case that was almost as big as the 'yacht' that was to carry it, and with no idea of what I was doing there. I decided, then and there, that I was going to enjoy this strange and unexpected adventure.

'Supper's ready,' Davies called from below.

I went down the ladder, and was astonished at the change in the cabin. All the luggage had been put away, and everything looked neat and comfortable. There were glasses on the table, and the smell of hot whisky and lemon hid the earlier unpleasant smells. Davies could see from my face that I had got over my bad mood, and he was obviously happier.

We sat smoking our pipes and talking for a while, and then came the problem of going to bed in the tiny cabin. After bumping my head and elbows several times, I finally managed it and lay down between the rough blankets.

Davies, moving quickly and easily, was soon in his bed. 'It's quite comfortable, isn't it?' he said, as he blew out the light.

I felt a drop of water on my face. 'I suppose the deck's not leaking?' I said, as politely as I could.

Davies was out of bed in a moment. 'I'll just put something over it for tonight,' he said, 'and I'll fix it in the morning. I've been doing some repairs but I must have missed that bit.'

In a few minutes he was back in bed, and soon after, I fell asleep.

2

A different kind of sailing

After a restless night in my uncomfortable bed, I was woken next morning by water pouring down on top of me. I sat up suddenly and hit my head on the ceiling.

'Sorry!' cried Davies cheerfully from above. 'I'm washing the deck. Come up and swim. Slept well?'

'Quite well,' I replied crossly, and stepped out of bed into a pool of water. But I went up on deck and, diving over the side, buried my stiffness and bad temper in the loveliest fiord of the lovely Baltic.

I climbed back on board, and while I was getting dressed on deck, I examined the *Dulcibella*. She seemed very small but was, in fact, ten metres long and three metres wide. She looked large enough for sailing weekends close to the shore, but I could not imagine how she had made the journey from England to the Baltic. She was not a beautiful boat, either, sitting low in the water, and with a very tall mast. But in spite of her plainness, she looked very solid and safe, and I was grateful for that.

Davies cooked a surprisingly good breakfast, better than my London cook ever managed. As soon as we had washed the dishes, he said, 'There's a good wind. Let's sail down the fiord,' and disappeared up on deck. I joined him there, trying to be of use, but he did not need me, or even notice me. He seemed to be everywhere at once, raising the sail, pulling on ropes, and steering the yacht, all at the same time. Soon the *Dulcibella* was turning away from the shore and sailing towards the open fiord.

11

I sat on deck, lazily watching the green fields and little white houses pass slowly by. With the clear blue sky, and the sun shining on the water, it was a beautiful view. I looked round at Davies. He had one brown arm on the helm, and seemed lost in his thoughts. For a moment I studied his face more closely than I had ever done before. I had never considered him worth spending much of my valuable time on, as I had always thought him very ordinary. Now I was beginning to see how wrong I had been. In that calm face I saw honesty, and bravery. Above all, he was sincere. I began to wonder how often I had misjudged other people in the past; I had always been so confident of choosing the right men to know.

Suddenly Davies threw me the chart. 'Just tell me which side of the buoy we should pass, will you?' he said. I looked in horror at the black marks on the paper, which meant nothing to me.

Soon he said, 'Never mind, I expect it's all deep water round here.'

In a minute we were passing the buoy, probably on the wrong side, since sand could clearly be seen below us. Then there was a loud unpleasant noise under the boat, and the *Dulcibella* ran aground.

With a little effort we managed to push her off the sandbank, but I felt horribly guilty, and apologized to Davies.

'You must remember I'm a complete fool when it comes to sailing,' I said. 'You'll have a lot to teach me. I've only ever sailed with a crew to do all the actual work.'

'Crew!' said Davies, shocked. 'Why, the whole fun of the thing is to do everything yourself.'

'Well, I've felt all morning that I'm no use to you.'

'I'm awfully sorry! But it's just the opposite – you may be all the use in the world when . . .' He did not finish, and became lost in his thoughts again.

That night we anchored in calm water in the shelter of the shore, and after supper I asked Davies to tell me about his voyage from England. He spread his charts on the table, and took his log-book from the shelf.

'There's not really much to tell,' he began. 'My friend Morrison and I left Dover on 6th August, and sailed to Ostend, and up the Dutch coast. Then we travelled through Holland by river and canal to Rotterdam, on to Amsterdam, and back into the North Sea. We sailed round the Zuyder Zee, then north to the Frisian Islands. Look, they stretch for a hundred and ninety kilometres from west to east, along the Dutch and German coast.'

He suddenly became enthusiastic. 'Look at this,' he said, pointing to an area covered with little black marks on the chart. 'It's all sand between the islands and the coast. There are channels through the sands but they're all wrong on the charts because the sands keep moving all the time. It's a wonderful place for sailing – no towns or harbours, just a few villages with a shop where you can get food. The islands themselves are really just big sandbanks, you see.'

'Isn't it rather dangerous sailing there?' I asked.

'Not if you know what you're doing,' he replied. 'The *Dulcibella* can sail in very shallow water. Of course, you can't help running aground sometimes. At high tide those sandbanks are all hidden – everything looks the same.'

'Didn't you ever take a pilot?' I asked.

'Pilot? Well, yes, I did take one once.'

'And what happened?'

'Oh! I ran aground, of course. It was stupid of me to follow him. I wonder what the weather's doing.' He climbed quickly up on deck.

'Rain coming,' he said, on his return. 'And possibly wind. But we're safe enough here. Time for bed, I think.'

'You haven't finished your story yet,' I said.

'Well, Morrison had to leave me when we got to Terschelling, the third island. I followed the Dutch islands eastwards to Borkum, the first of the German islands.'

'When was that?' I asked.

'About the 9th of September.'

'You haven't finished your story yet,' I said.

14

'That's only two weeks before you wrote to me,' I said. 'You were quick getting to Flensburg.'

'Yes. I went to Norderney, the third German island, but then decided to go straight for the Baltic. So I sailed to the Eider River, took the canal to Kiel on the Baltic, then turned north for Flensburg. I was a week there, getting repairs done, and then you came, and here we are. And now we really must go to bed. We'll have a fine sail tomorrow.'

He ended with rather forced cheerfulness, and quickly rolled up the chart. He had cut short the description of the last part of his journey. Why, I wondered? Perhaps he did not want me to realize how dangerous a voyage it had been. Whatever the reason, there was some mystery about it, and I wanted to know more.

'Tell me about the passage to the Eider River,' I said. 'That was rather a long one, wasn't it?'

'About a hundred and twelve kilometres, I suppose.'

'Didn't you stop anywhere?'

'Only once. I took shelter behind one of the sandbanks one night. Oh,' he added, 'I didn't fix that hole in the deck above your bed. I'd better do that before the rain comes. You go to bed.'

He disappeared. While I prepared for bed, I wondered again what he was hiding from me. I heard hammering above my head, and then he reappeared and got into bed.

'I say, do you think you'll like this sort of thing?' he said.

'If the scenery's as beautiful as it was today, I shall.'

'Ah, yes! The scenery,' he said quietly. 'You must think I'm odd, liking the Frisian Islands so much. How would you like sailing among those sandbanks?'

'I should hate it,' I replied, sleepily. 'Did you ever see another yacht there?'

'Only one,' he said. 'Good night.'
'Good night.'

Early next day, we raised the sails and the *Dulcibella* made her way into the fiord, where the wind was blowing the sea into short sharp waves, and I began to enjoy my first day of real sailing.

Again that night, we turned back to the shore, where we anchored. Among the trees, only a hundred metres away, we could see a little monument. We took the dinghy to investigate. It was a monument to those who had died in the war between Germany and Denmark, when the area became German. It was very simple, but, in the moonlight and the peace of the evening, it was very moving too.

'Germany's a great nation,' said Davies quietly. 'I wonder if we shall ever have to fight her.'

During supper we talked about war, and especially war at sea. This was Davies's hobby and he knew a lot about it. When he took a book from the shelf, I saw that his books were all about war at sea, or sailing in small boats.

Looking at the books reminded me that I wanted to read his log-book, so, while Davies was washing the dishes, I took it down and began to read. There was much detailed description of winds, tides, and distances travelled each day. I turned to the later part, about his voyage to the Baltic. The log-book reached the 9th September, then the next page jumped to the 13th, and described the following three days with only the most basic details:

> *13th Sept.* Decided to go to the Baltic. Sailed 4.00 a.m.
> Fair west-north-west wind. Anchored for night in the
> shelter of Hohenhörn sandbank.
> *14th Sept.* Nothing.

15th Sept. East wind. West by south 6 km, north-east
by north 24 km. Arrived Eider River 11.30.

I then noticed a page had been torn out of the book, between the
9th and 13th, and realized that the entries from the 13th to the
15th had all been written at the same time. Clearly, the log-book
had been changed after the event – but why? And what event?

I decided not to ask Davies about it, feeling unwilling to force
a confession from him. After all, I thought, it was probably
nothing of any great importance.

Before going to bed, we went up on deck and stood, listening
to the wind in the trees. 'The wind is sure to move round to the
north soon,' said Davies. 'I asked some fishermen about duck
shooting, and they said the best place would be Schlei Fiord.
That's about twenty kilometres south, on the way to Kiel. We
need a north wind for that.'

'I don't mind where we go,' I said.

'You mean anywhere in the Baltic?' asked Davies.

'Yes. Anywhere round here,' I said. We stood for a while,
looking at the moonlight on the water. Then we went below.

I had told Davies that I wanted to learn to sail the yacht in all
sorts of weather, so he made me work hard for the next two days.
I learnt how to steer the yacht in a high wind, when to take the
sails in, when to let them out, how to deal with the little storms
that blew up the fiords. I learnt to work with ropes that were wet
and stiff, and to tell the depth of water by using the lead line.

On the second day, I heard the sound of ducks and, looking
up, I saw about twenty of them, flying in a V-shape across our
path. 'You see,' I cried. 'There *are* ducks here.'

'Yes,' Davies said doubtfully, 'but I've heard it's difficult to

17

get permission to shoot them here.' He paused, then without looking at me, he added, 'If we were in the North Sea, among the Frisian Islands, we wouldn't need permission.'

'You surely don't want to leave the Baltic?' I cried.

'Why not?' he asked.

'But, be sensible, man,' I said crossly. 'It's almost October, the summer's over, and the good weather's finished. Every yacht like ours is back in harbour for the winter. We've had the good luck to find these lovely fiords to sail in, and we've just seen there are ducks here. Why on earth make a long and dangerous voyage back to those islands in the North Sea?'

'It wouldn't be very dangerous,' he replied.

'But what *for*? What's the *point* . . .?' I was beginning to lose my patience, and was about to say something that would have ended our holiday there and then, but Davies spoke first.

'I'm sorry, old man,' he said with a smile. 'I'm being awfully selfish. You've been a real friend coming all this way to join me. Let's get to Schlei Fiord and ask about the ducks. We must be almost there.'

We soon found the narrow entrance to the fiord and the pilot's little white house, where the fishermen had told Davies to ask about duck shooting. The pilot was very helpful, and told us the best places to look for ducks.

Davies and I were friends again by the time we returned to the *Dulcibella*, and all thoughts of going to the Frisian Islands seemed forgotten. I went to bed, hoping for the chance of some duck shooting the next day, and expecting no more excitement than a sudden fierce storm blowing up the fiord. I had no way of knowing that my autumn holiday was about to turn into a very different kind of experience.

3

The missing page in the log-book

Next morning, we found the *Dulcibella* wrapped in thick fog, which meant, of course, that nothing could be done until it lifted. After breakfast, we heard someone on deck, and a short, grey-haired man appeared in the cabin doorway.

'Bartels!' cried Davies. 'Was that the *Johannes* that I heard arrive last night? Have some coffee.' He spoke in his very poor German. 'This is my friend, Carruthers. Captain Bartels of the *Johannes*,' he added to me, and went to make some coffee.

Bartels said quietly to me, 'It is good for Captain Davies to have a friend with him. He is a fine young man, but he is too brave, he takes too many risks.'

'Where did you meet?' I asked, interested.

'In an ugly place, in ugly weather,' he replied, very seriously. 'Has he not told you?'

Here it was again, the suggestion of some mystery, some dangerous event that I did not know about. I decided there and then to ask Davies to tell me the truth.

Just then he came back. 'Bartels helped me out of a bit of trouble in the North Sea, didn't you, Bartels?'

'It was nothing,' said Bartels. 'But I've told you before, Captain, the North Sea is no place for your little boat at this time of the year.'

He drank his coffee, and before he went, he advised Davies in a fatherly way to think again about going home before the winter began. Davies went with him back to his own boat, but returned at once, and sat down opposite me in the cabin. I think he knew what was coming.

'What did he mean?' I asked.

'I'll tell you,' said Davies. 'I'll tell you the whole thing. It's a kind of confession, I suppose. It's been worrying me a lot, and perhaps you'll be able to help me. But it's for you to decide.' He paused for a second. 'Something happened when I was in the Frisian Islands that I haven't told you about.'

'It began near Norderney,' I said. 'About the 9th September.'

'How did you guess that?' he asked in surprise.

'You're not very good at hiding things,' I replied. 'Go on.'

'Well, you're right. Norderney. I'd been asking the local people about ducks, and they told me I should ask a German called Dollmann, with a big yacht, who did a lot of shooting. On the 9th September I came across his yacht, the *Medusa*. She was very big, very smart too – new paint, and a crew in uniform. I decided to go and speak to him.'

'Just a minute,' I said. 'Let's have a look at the chart.'

'Here's Norderney,' he said, spreading out the chart. 'There's a harbour at the west end of the island, the only real harbour on the islands. The *Medusa* was anchored near it and I rowed over after dinner, and was taken to the main cabin. It was very grand. Dollmann was finishing dinner.'

'What was he like?' I asked.

'About fifty, tall and thin, with grey hair and a short grey beard,' replied Davies. 'I asked about the duck shooting, and he said that there was none at all. But he wanted to know all about me and what I was doing there. We talked for a long time and he was quite friendly when I left. I intended to sail on eastwards next day, but Dollmann came to visit me on the *Dulcibella*, and

From the Baltic to the Frisian Islands

Baltic Sea

Flensburg

Kiel

Kiel Ship Canal

River Eider

Brunsbüttel

Cuxhaven

HAMBURG

River Elbe

GERMANY

Bremen

River Weser

Scharhörn

Hohenhörn Sandbank

River Jade

Wilhelmshaven

Wangeroog

Spiekeroog

Langeoog

Bensersiel

Baltrum

Norderney

Juist

Emden

Memmert

River Ems

Borkum

GERMAN FRISIAN ISLANDS

North Sea

HOLLAND

then invited me to dinner on the *Medusa* a couple of times. In the end I stayed three more days anchored at Norderney.'

'How did you spend your time?' I asked.

'Well, we talked, and – er – I met his daughter two or three times. I hadn't seen her that first evening.'

'What was she like?' I asked.

'Oh! A very nice girl,' he replied, turning a little pink. 'Finally, we left Norderney together. Dollmann said the Baltic would be better for duck shooting. We agreed to sail together as far as Cuxhaven. He was sailing to Hamburg and I was going to take the new ship canal to Kiel. It's about a hundred kilometres from Norderney to Cuxhaven.'

Davies paused, looking at the chart. 'We left on the morning of 13th September,' he began again. 'The weather was bad, and there was a strong wind from the north-west. It was nothing for a big yacht like his, of course, but I soon realized I had been a fool to set out. After Wangeroog, the last of the islands, the wind got really strong, but it was too late to turn back by then. The sand stretches twenty-five kilometres from Cuxhaven right out to the Scharhörn, so you have to go round the Scharhörn to reach Cuxhaven, and I knew the sea would be extremely rough there. Suddenly I saw the *Medusa* was waiting for me to get closer. As I reached her, Dollmann shouted to me, slowly and clearly, "It's too rough for you to go round the Scharhörn. Follow me. I'll show you a short cut through the sandbanks."'

Davies paused, to point out the places on the chart. 'Look, here's the Telte, it's a wide channel through the sands. It's all right if you know your way, but later on it's cut in two by the Hohenhörn sandbank, and it gets very shallow and difficult. Dollmann seemed to know what he was doing, so, after a

22

moment's thought, I held up my arm to show that I would follow him. You asked me if I ever took a pilot. That was the only time.'

Davies spoke bitterly. 'I followed him into the Telte channel, but then I saw he wasn't waiting for me. The *Medusa* was sailing much faster than I could, and soon disappeared into the mist and rain. There was nothing I could do. I couldn't turn round and go back. At high tide, as it was then, all the sand is covered, so you can't see the sandbanks or the channels, and there are no buoys. The wind was behind me too, and was very strong by this time. It was driving me straight on to the Hohenhörn sandbank.

'Suddenly I saw the waves breaking on the Hohenhörn right in front of me. I tried to steer along the edge of the sandbank, hoping to find a way through. But the wind carried the *Dulcibella* violently on to the sandbank. The next wave carried me further on to the bank and into a little channel. I can't describe the next few minutes. My hand had been hurt, and the helm damaged, in that first bump, and I had no control over the boat. The waves were crashing all around me, and finally I ran aground.'

Davies shook his head. 'I was so angry with myself, you can't imagine. I couldn't do anything because my hand was useless. But that's when Bartels saw me and came to help. He'd taken shelter in a deeper part of the channel that I was in. He saw I was in difficulties, so he and his boy rowed across to me. They soon had the sails down, and pulled me away from the sand and down the channel, to where the *Johannes* lay. He's a good man, Bartels. If it weren't for him, I wouldn't be here now.

'The next day he helped me repair the damage to the helm. He was sailing for the Eider River and on to the Baltic that way. It's longer than going by the new ship canal but both routes come

'The wind carried the Dulcibella *violently on to the sandbank.'*

out at Kiel. I went with him, and three days later I was in the Baltic. I wrote to you a week after I got there. You see, by then I had realized that *Dollmann was a spy.*'

He said it very simply, and I stared at him in astonishment.

'A spy?' I said. 'What do you mean? A spy of what – of whom?'

'Well, I'm not sure that "spy" is the right word, but he's

something very bad. He deliberately tried to make me go aground, you see. He tried to kill me.'

'Are you sure?' It was difficult to believe it.

'Oh yes!' said Davies calmly. 'I've worked it all out. Dollmann knew his way through the sands, by the Telte channel, and his yacht was big enough to manage it. You see, the Telte divides into two before the Hohenhörn sandbank. Dollmann turned north and then into the channel that goes around the Hohenhörn. But before he turned, he led me straight for the sandbank. And he deliberately left me behind, so I didn't know that he had turned. He meant me to keep going straight ahead. I should have been broken to pieces on the Hohenhörn.'

'Why weren't you?' I asked.

Davies pointed again at the chart. 'Look,' he said. 'The Telte divides into two quite big channels, which go round the Hohenhörn to the north and the south. But there's also a very narrow channel that goes through the middle. It's so small that I hadn't noticed it, when I looked at the chart before we sailed. That's the one I was carried into. If I had been on the sandbank, the *Dulcibella* would have broken up in three minutes. I was just lucky that day.'

Lucky – and brave, I thought to myself. 'But what makes you think he's a spy?' I asked. 'Perhaps he was in difficulties too, and lost sight of you by accident?'

Davies shook his head. 'Look at it from the beginning,' he said. 'The first time I met Dollmann, he asked me all sorts of questions about what I was doing and why. I was terribly enthusiastic about my voyage and talked quite freely. I told him that I was exploring the channels between the islands, working out all the movements of the sandbanks, and making notes about

25

it all, because the English charts were so hopelessly out of date.

'After that he did his best to get rid of me. He said there were no ducks, that the Baltic was very good for sailing and for ducks, and he offered to show me the way. He wanted to get me away from those islands. I don't think he meant to kill me at first, but when the chance came later on, he just took it.'

'But what about his crew?' I asked. 'Surely they would have noticed.'

'There wasn't anyone else on deck, when he told me about the short cut. He was steering the *Medusa* himself.'

'And his daughter? Do you think she wanted to get rid of you, too?'

Davies's face suddenly went very red. 'I'm sure she knew nothing about it,' he said fiercely. He began trying to light his pipe again, and I thought I could guess another reason why he had agreed to sail with Dollmann.

'Let's look at it from Dollmann's point of view,' I said. 'A German finds an Englishman exploring the German coast, and checking the charts. Perhaps he thought *you* were the spy.'

'But that's just the point,' cried Davies. '*He's not German.* He's an Englishman.'

'An Englishman!'

'Yes, I'm sure of it,' said Davies. 'Every time I spoke to him on the *Medusa* he spoke German. He said he only knew a few words of English. And when he offered to show me the short cut through the sands, he shouted in German. Now, you know that I never like taking a pilot, so I hesitated before agreeing. He must have thought I hadn't understood him, so he shouted again, only this time in English, without any German accent.'

'And if he was planning to lead you to your death on the

Hohenhörn,' I said, 'it wouldn't matter if you guessed that he wasn't German!'

'That's right,' agreed Davies eagerly. 'I knew you'd understand. I'm sure he's an Englishman, working for the German government and giving them information. He's been living here for years, and has a house on Norderney. Oh! And I met a friend of his, a Commander von Brüning, in the German navy. He came on board the *Medusa* one day when I was there. He's captain of the gunboat *Blitz*, on guard duty for the fishing boats around the islands.'

'Did von Brüning seem to know Dollmann well?'

'Yes, very well,' replied Davies. 'Now,' he continued, 'let me explain what I think is happening.'

He took down a map of Germany from the shelf and spread it on the table. 'Look at Germany. It's the strongest nation in Europe, and it's led by the young Kaiser, who's a great man for getting things done. Their industry is growing very fast and, in order to have markets for what they produce, they need colonies. To get and keep these colonies, and to protect their shipping, they need a strong navy. They have only a small one at present, but it's very good, and they're building more ships as fast as they can. In Britain we already have a strong navy, because we live on an island, and we need to protect the sea routes between us and our colonies. Most of our food comes to us by sea. If we lose control of the sea, we're finished. But Germany is in the very centre of Europe, and can get all she needs from her neighbours. She has the biggest army in the world. She can already compete with our industry, and soon she may be able to compete with our navy. And unfortunately, we're not ready for her. All our naval bases are on the south coast, opposite our old enemy, France. We have no bases in the North Sea. We should realize that Germany is the danger now, and do something about it.'

Davies paused and looked at me anxiously. 'These are not just my ideas, you know. Other people worry about this too.'

'Yes, I know,' I said. 'But go on.'

Davies pointed at the map again. 'Now look at the coast of Germany. It's very short and it's cut in two by Denmark. Most of the German coast is on the Baltic, which is not much use to them as it's too far from the Atlantic. That's why the Kaiser has built the new ship canal from Kiel to the River Elbe, so that he can move his ships from the Baltic to the North Sea quickly. The North Sea coast is the important one but it's very short – three hundred kilometres at the most. And not all of it can be used. Most of the coastline is hidden behind sandbanks, or a line of islands. There's just one wide opening, with the mouths of the three big rivers, the Elbe, the Weser, and the Jade, leading to Hamburg, Bremen, and Wilhelmshaven. The important bit of coast is the hundred and twelve kilometres from Borkum to the Elbe, and that's the part that Dollmann stopped me exploring.'

He paused again, looking at the sandbanks shown on the map. 'If England were at war with Germany,' he added, slowly and seriously, 'the whole of that coast would be important, sands and all. There are channels through those sands that can only be used by small ships like Bartels' *Johannes*. In wartime the main sea routes to Hamburg and the other ports would be carefully guarded. But if we knew where the channels through the sands were, small gunboats could use them to attack German ships in the mouths of the big rivers. And, of course, German gunboats could use them to attack our ships off the coast. Then they could disappear among the sands, where our ships would be too big to follow them. All our warships need deep water to sail in, and can't possibly use those channels.'

'I see,' I said. I began to understand what Davies was trying to tell me. 'So German gunboats could travel through the sands from Hamburg to Holland, and our North Sea ships couldn't get near them.'

'That's right,' said Davies. 'Or of course, our gunboats could do the trip the other way, if we knew where the channels were. The trouble is, we don't know. None of our fishing boats use these waters and our charts are years out of date. It just happens that I enjoy sailing in waters like these and bringing the charts up to date.'

'I'm not surprised Dollmann wanted to get rid of you,' I said.

'Yes,' agreed Davies. 'But I'd like to know just what Dollmann is doing there.'

'It must be something very important if he's prepared to kill you,' I said. 'And there's only one way to find out.'

Davies jumped up in excitement and hit his head on the cabin ceiling. 'You mean you'll come?' he cried.

'Of course,' I said. 'We'll have to go back to Norderney to find out why an Englishman is watching those waters and keeping other people out of them. When do we start?'

'We can go back to the North Sea through the ship canal from Kiel,' said Davies. 'We could start for Kiel at once. The fog's lifting and there's a little south-west wind.'

'How far is it?' I asked. 'It'll mean sailing all night!'

'It's only about forty kilometres,' he replied. 'I know it's not the best wind we could have, but we ought to take the chance.'

It was hopeless arguing about winds with Davies, so we set off lunchless, but full of excitement.

4

The pathfinders

We arrived at Kiel at one o'clock in the morning, and the next day we made our preparations for exploring the North Sea sandbanks. We bought food, oil, and plenty of warm clothes, and I wrote to my boss at the Foreign Office, requesting another week or two of holiday. I asked him to send his reply to me at the post office in Norderney, as Davies and I had no fixed address. When we were ready, we sailed the *Dulcibella* through the huge iron gates of the ship canal that connects Germany's two seas, the North Sea and the Baltic. For two days, with some of the largest ships in the world, we travelled slowly through the great waterway, wondering at the engineering and organizational ability of the nation that had created it.

When we reached Brunsbüttel, at the North Sea end of the canal, Davies went off to buy fresh milk. Meanwhile, an official came on board to examine our papers.

'*Dulcibella*,' he said. 'Someone from a big yacht was asking about you the day before yesterday.'

'Did he say what he wanted?' I asked.

'Not "he", Captain. It was a young lady,' replied the official. He smiled knowingly. 'She wanted to know if you had gone through the canal. It's a pity you missed her.'

'Well, we'll probably see her in Hamburg,' I said.

'No, she was going into the North Sea.'

'Did she say where?' I asked.

'No,' he answered. 'But don't worry, Captain. There are

plenty of pretty girls in Hamburg.' He laughed, and went on to the next boat, as Davies returned with the milk.

Then the great gates opened, and we turned the *Dulcibella* towards the North Sea.

'Well, Davies,' I said, when I told him what the official had said, 'Dollmann can't believe he's got rid of you, if he sent his daughter to enquire after you like that.'

'I don't think he sent her to ask,' said Davies. 'I think it was her own idea to find out.' He had a strange look on his face, half happy, half confused.

With the strong tide, we soon reached Cuxhaven. Davies's plan was to explore the sandbanks between the Scharhörn and Cuxhaven, to find the channels and put them on his charts. Soon I realized that banks of yellow and brown sand were appearing to the west of us. Davies was looking delighted, as we left the main channel and sailed westwards, straight for the sandbanks.

'Centreboard up,' he cried. 'Now for some real sailing!'

We were in an extremely narrow channel. While I measured the depth of the water with the lead line, and called out the metres, Davies steered, pulled in the sails, and kept an eye on the chart. But in spite of our carefulness, there was a bumping sound from below, and we ran aground.

'There's nothing to worry about,' Davies said cheerfully. 'When the tide rises, we'll float off the sandbank. This is a good moment to have lunch.'

When we went back on deck, it was low tide, and the yacht was sitting on the top of a sandbank. As far as the eye could see, there was nothing but sand, broken here and there by the winding path of a channel. Some of these channels still held water, but others had dried out completely. Under a dull grey sky, the wind blew across this wide empty space, crying softly like a child in pain. It seemed the saddest, loneliest place on earth.

Davies, however, had climbed the mast and was examining the sand enthusiastically. His face shone with pleasure. I had never seen him look happier.

'There!' he cried. 'You see what I mean? Have you ever seen anything like this?' He climbed down and then jumped down on to the sandbank. 'Come on!' he called. 'The only way to understand a place like this is to explore it at low tide.'

I joined him, and together we ran over the sandbanks as fast as our heavy rubber boots would let us. Davies noted down every post or marker, and every bend in the channels, on his chart.

'Right!' he said when he had finished. 'Now let's get back to the *Dulcibella*. This tide's rising fast.'

We turned, and ran for the yacht. I was thankful to reach it in time, before the sands were completely covered by the incoming tide. I stood on deck, and watched the sea making its way across the desert of sand. Under my feet the *Dulcibella* gave a jump, paused, gave another jump, and was suddenly floating again on the grey waters, which now hid the wide area of sand where Davies and I had just walked.

We raised the sail and set off, following the channel we had just explored. All around us stretched the sea, with nothing to show where the channel was. I felt completely lost, but Davies was his usual confident self. He made me call out the depth of water every few seconds, while he steered carefully, feeling for the edge of the sandbank.

It was getting dark. The German coast had already disappeared, and the sea all around us looked exactly the same to me. But I knew that Davies carried a picture in his head of the

complicated pattern of the sands around and beneath us, which
he had already charted.

'Right! Let go the anchor,' he said at last, 'and lower the sails.'

'Where are we?' I asked.

'In the shelter of the Hohenhörn, in the channel where Bartels

'Let's get back to the Dulcibella. *This tide's rising fast.'*

took me that night. If you listen, you can hear the waves breaking on the Hohenhörn, where I went aground.'

And sure enough, we could hear the waves crashing on the sandbank. As darkness fell, the wind grew fiercer, and the sea rougher. This was the first time we had anchored at night out of sight of land, and I found it a frightening experience as the *Dulcibella* rolled from side to side and the sea thundered on the sandbank. But I knew now that Davies was a yachtsman of extraordinary skill, and if he said that we were perfectly safe, then safe we were.

Nothing happened in the next ten days to disturb us at our work. We spent all the daylight hours exploring the sandbanks and channels around Cuxhaven, and marking the changes on the charts. We found nothing to explain why Dollmann wanted to get rid of Davies, and nobody asked questions or tried to stop us.

'I'm sure it's something to do with these channels through the sands,' said Davies at last. 'But nobody seems to mind our being here. The answer to the riddle must be near where I first met Dollmann, at Norderney.'

So we left the Cuxhaven area, and set sail for the Frisian Islands. Helped by a strong easterly wind, we sailed all the way without stopping. We reached the island of Wangeroog just before dark, and ran the *Dulcibella* aground on the sand a hundred metres from the shore. There were three fishing boats anchored about a kilometre from us. Davies set out on foot across the sand to get fresh water and oil, leaving me alone on the yacht.

'Make sure you keep the light burning on the mast,' he said as he left. 'It's my only guide back to the yacht.'

It had been an exhausting day and I was feeling very tired, so

I lay down on the seat in the cabin. I was half asleep when I heard footsteps on the sand outside, and then a voice calling in German, 'Hello there, on the yacht!'

I was wide awake in a second, and sat up and listened. The call came again, 'Hello there, on the yacht!'

I did not reply. Was this, I wondered, something to do with the mystery? I heard someone climb onto the deck of the *Dulcibella*. Suddenly the light on the mast went out. The visitor walked along the deck to the doorway, and began to climb down the ladder into the cabin. I should have waited until he was down, but I was too eager to catch him. I jumped towards the ladder and caught hold of a leg. My unknown visitor kicked out, pulled himself free, and reached the deck, leaving me holding a boot. I rushed up on deck after him, but he was too fast for me, and I did not manage to catch him. I thought of Davies coming back with the oil and water, unable to find the yacht, so I quickly relit the mast light.

When Davies returned, I told him about our visitor.

'I think we're being watched,' I said, 'unless he was just a thief, from one of those fishing boats, perhaps.'

'I don't think the local Germans would steal from a yacht,' replied Davies. 'And they wouldn't put out the mast light. They're all seamen and know how important it is.'

We discussed what to do. The charts we were using, with all our corrections and notes, were the only things anyone might want to see, so we decided to hide them and the log-book. Now if anyone came on board, they would think we were just two harmless young men, on an autumn sailing holiday.

We sat up late looking at the chart. There were seven islands in the German Frisian group, separated from the coast by the sands, which were mostly dry at low tide. There were small villages, just a few houses and a church, on most of the islands. Norderney had the only harbour. It was quite a busy little seaside town in the summer, but it was almost empty for the rest of the year. The mainland had no large towns either, just a few small villages. Davies pointed to the row of islands on the chart.

'Just look at the fine, sheltered harbour hidden between these islands and the coast! It's fifty kilometres long and ten kilometres wide, perfect for small gunboats.'

'Have you noticed,' I asked, 'that on the mainland there's a

My unknown visitor pulled himself free, leaving me holding a boot.

channel or a stream leading to each of those villages on the coast? Shouldn't we explore those too?'

'I don't think so,' he replied. 'They only lead to those tiny villages.' Davies hated spending time on land.

'Yes, but look, ' I said, pointing to the chart, 'there are small harbours at Bensersiel and other villages.'

'So there are,' said Davies. 'They're probably just big enough for the local fishing boats.'

'Perhaps we should have a look at them,' I said.

'Perhaps,' he agreed unwillingly. 'But there's a lot more real work to be done further out, among the islands.'

We spent the next day exploring the channels around Wangeroog. There was only one of the fishing boats still there, and as we passed, I saw it was called the *Kormoran*. Later in the afternoon, we caught sight of a small grey naval ship, moving slowly past, outside the islands.

'The *Blitz*,' said Davies. 'Von Brüning's ship.'

As it happened, we went to Bensersiel sooner than we had expected. Two days later a strong south-west wind began to blow, promising storms to follow. We saw that the *Blitz* had already taken shelter, and was now anchored just south of Spiekeroog, next to several fishing boats. During the afternoon, the wind went round to the north-east – a bad sign, Davies said – and the sky turned black, bringing violent rainstorms. We decided to shelter at Bensersiel and had an exciting run through the sandbanks and a very rough sea to the shore, where with great skill Davies managed to bring us safely into the tiny harbour. He, of course, always preferred to anchor for the night away from the shore, but I was glad to step on to dry land, after more than two weeks at sea.

5

A meeting and a warning

I slept very comfortably that night, and was woken by the sound of Davies talking in his limited German to someone on the shore. When he came on board, he told me that he had met Commander von Brüning, who had invited us to have a drink in the village pub with him at twelve o'clock.

Davies had another piece of news. 'The *Kormoran* is here in harbour too. It must have been them watching us, surely? And then passing the information on to von Brüning.'

'Almost certainly von Brüning wants to know more about us,' I said. 'We must be very careful what we say to him. Perhaps he'll come on board and ask to see our log.'

'In that case we must show it to him. Let's be open about it! I hate hiding things, anyway.'

And so we decided on an important change of plan, to bring our log and charts out of their hiding-place, and be as honest as we could. But just how much did von Brüning know? Did he know that we had not fired a shot at a single duck in the North Sea, and that we had explored the sands all along the coast? Did he know about Dollmann's attempt to get rid of Davies, and Davies's lucky escape? We could not tell. So it would be safer to tell the truth as far as possible in the coming interview.

But first we tried to find out something about the *Kormoran*, so after breakfast we went for a walk round the village. The people were very friendly, and we stopped to talk to two of the fishermen. We asked them about the boats in the harbour, and they told us that the *Kormoran* was not a local fishing boat.

'She's from Memmert,' they said. 'She's trying to raise an old French ship, loaded with gold, that sank off Juist. Her captain, Herr Grimm, is in charge of the work. That's him over there.' They pointed to a man standing on the bridge across the little stream that ran into the harbour.

We walked out on the sand to inspect this channel, and then walked slowly back. 'Don't forget,' I said, 'when we talk to von Brüning, just be yourself. You need only tell one lie, about the trick Dollmann played you.'

'All right, I'll leave you to do most of the talking. Look, there's Grimm again. Look at his boots as we pass him.' When we did, we saw that Grimm was wearing *shoes*, though of course that did not prove he had left one of his boots on the *Dulcibella*.

It was a few minutes after twelve when we entered the village pub. Davies introduced me to Commander von Brüning, and we sat down and ordered something to drink. I must say, I liked von Brüning as soon as I saw him. He was tall, with fair hair and a short beard. His eyes were blue and friendly, but extremely intelligent. I was glad we had decided to tell the truth – the commander was not a man you could trick easily. We had decided that Davies should ask immediately about Dollmann, his supposed friend. I was horrified to see Davies's face go pink as he asked his question in German, but then I remembered an obvious reason for his embarrassment. I had to make sure, however, that von Brüning also understood the reason for the embarrassment.

'He's still away,' replied von Brüning, 'but his yacht is back at Norderney. His daughter must be there too.'

'She's a very fine boat,' said Davies, his face getting even redder. Von Brüning smiled, looking thoughtfully at Davies. I saw a chance, and took it pitilessly.

'Oh good, we can call on Fräulein Dollmann,' I said to Davies, smiling meaningfully at von Brüning at the same time. Davies looked even more miserable.

'But you have seen Herr Dollmann since I have, surely?' said von Brüning. 'Didn't you sail to the Elbe with him?'

'Only part of the way,' replied Davies. 'The *Medusa* was too fast for me.'

'Oh, yes! I remember,' said von Brüning. 'The weather was very bad that day. I thought you would have trouble round the Scharhörn.'

'We didn't go round the Scharhörn,' said Davies. 'Dollmann showed me a short cut through the sands, but I lost him and ran aground.'

'Where was this?' asked von Brüning.

'On the Hohenhörn,' said Davies simply.

The commander's smile disappeared and his eyes opened wide. His surprise was so obvious that I was sure he had heard nothing of this before.

'You mean Dollmann took you through the Telte channel in that sort of weather and you ran aground on the Hohenhörn? Is that where you lost him?'

'No, he had already disappeared in the rain,' replied Davies. 'He couldn't have seen what happened. Anyway, it didn't matter. The tide was rising and I soon floated off. But I decided to spend the night in the shelter of the sandbank.'

'Didn't they wait for you at the ship canal?' asked von Brüning.

'I didn't go that way,' Davies replied. 'The wind was against it, so I sailed to the Eider River and on to the Baltic that way.'

Commander von Brüning laughed suddenly and turned to me. 'Really,' he said, 'your friend amuses me. He has the most terrifying adventures, and makes them sound perfectly ordinary.'

'That's nothing to him,' I said. 'He prefers it. He anchored us the other day behind the Hohenhörn in a horrible wind; said it was safer than a harbour and much cleaner.'

'I'm surprised he didn't decide this storm was just the wind he needed to sail to England,' said von Brüning.

'There was no pilot to follow, you see,' I said, with a smile.

'And no pretty daughter,' laughed the commander.

Davies frowned and looked so angry with me that I decided to say no more about Dollmann's daughter. I suddenly thought that if Grimm was working with von Brüning, the commander would know about the *Dulcibella's* night-time visitor. It would seem strange if we said nothing about it.

So I said, 'By the way, I thought the local people were honest, but we had a thief on the yacht the other night.'

'Really?' he replied. 'They're excellent people, but in the old days they used to take things from wrecks on this coast, so it's a way of life for them. They probably thought the *Dulcibella* was deserted.'

'Talking about wrecks,' I said, 'isn't there one round here that's supposed to be full of French gold? Is that true?'

'Quite true,' said von Brüning. 'The *Corinne*. She sank in 1811 off the island of Juist with gold on board to pay Napoleon's army – in English money it would be worth about one and a half million pounds.'

'Has anyone found it?' I asked.

'They found the wreck years ago, but it had broken up and

41

the gold, being heavy, had sunk to the bottom. Several people have tried to find it but, of course, these sands keep moving all the time, so it's very difficult. Now a local company is trying. They're working from Memmert, an island near here. Herr Dollmann is one of the directors of the company. There's an engineer from Bremen involved, too – he comes from time to time.'

'And have they had any luck?' I asked.

'Not yet, but I hope they will. I've put a little money into the company myself.'

'Oh, dear!' I said. 'I hope I haven't been asking too many questions.'

'Not at all,' von Brüning laughed. 'It's no secret. Everyone on these islands knows all about it.'

The conversation continued, and he went on to find out from us, in the most natural yet skilful way, every detail of our explorations so far. As we talked, I was glad we had decided on telling the truth as far as possible, and gladder still that Davies was the man he was, eager, sincere, and completely believable.

'You speak very good German, Herr Carruthers,' said von Brüning at one point in the conversation.

'I've spent some time studying in Germany,' I replied.

'For your profession?' he asked.

'Yes,' I replied. 'I work in the Foreign Office.' I would have preferred not to have given him that information, but there was probably a letter from my boss, with a Foreign Office stamp, waiting for me at Norderney post office. My name was known, and we were watched. So the letter might be opened.

'When do you have to be back at work?' he asked.

'Next week, but I'm hoping my boss will agree to give me a

little more time,' I said. 'I've asked him to write to me at Norderney.'

'I see. And Herr Davies?'

'Oh! He's a free man,' I said. 'He'll sail around these islands until Christmas, I expect. So we're in no hurry.'

'I like this coast,' said Davies. 'And – we want to shoot some ducks.'

'You'll never find them,' said von Brüning, 'without a local man to guide you. I can easily find you a good man—'

'It's very kind of you, commander,' I said, 'but we'd better get to Norderney first, to collect my post and see if I can stay longer or not.'

'I'll be at Norderney myself very soon. Come and visit me there, will you? I'd like to show you the *Blitz*.'

'Thanks very much,' Davies and I said together, as warmly as we could manage.

As we were leaving, von Brüning took me on one side.

'One word in private with you, Herr Carruthers,' he said quietly. 'It's about the Dollmanns. You know how your friend feels. I wouldn't encourage him, if I were you. Herr Dollmann came here three years ago, but we know very little about him or his background.'

'I thought the Dollmanns were friends of yours,' I said.

'I know them, but I know everybody. I speak only as someone who wishes your friend well, you understand. I think you should forget about calling on the family in Norderney. That's all, just a warning.'

He gave me a long, serious look, and I could see that he was not going to say any more.

'Thanks. I'll remember,' I said.

43

'One word in private with you, Herr Carruthers,'
von Brüning said quietly.

The questions in my mind were, 'How much do you know, and what do you mean?' But I could not ask them.

Davies and I walked back to the yacht in silence, and went down to the cabin.

'Where exactly is Memmert?' I asked. Davies unrolled the chart and pointed at it. Then he threw himself on one of the seats, where he lay for some time, deep in thought.

South of the island of Juist, and running right up to the mouth of the River Ems, there is a large sandbank. Its western edge remains uncovered at high tide, forming a small island, about three kilometres long, and from two hundred to five hundred metres wide. This island is Memmert. The chart showed only one building, which I guessed was the centre for Dollmann's company. The island stands on the deep water channel of the Ems, providing a shelter for ships to anchor, even at low tide.

I thought hard about our conversation with von Brüning. Was he giving friendly advice to two young men on holiday, or a serious warning to two foreign spies? Perhaps he could not decide which we were. I was sure von Brüning had not known about Dollmann's attempt to kill Davies. He had guessed it, of course, when Davies told him about the short cut through the Telte channel.

The story of the French wreck and its gold provided a very good reason for Dollmann, Grimm, and von Brüning to be seen together, and to spend time on Memmert, especially as von Brüning had put money into the company. I was curious about Memmert. The more I thought about it, the more I believed that it might help us to solve the riddle.

Davies had still not spoken. He was annoyed with me, and

I knew why. But I was annoyed with him too. There was an important piece of the puzzle that he had not told me about. I was waiting for him to speak first but, in the end, his silence was too much for me, and I had to break it.

'Look, Davies,' I said, 'I'm sorry I mentioned you and Fräulein Dollmann.' No answer. I tried again, 'I couldn't help it, you know.'

At last Davies spoke. 'I don't know why you had to tell von Brüning everything. I just don't understand it.'

'You're being very unreasonable,' I replied. 'We agreed the best thing to do was to tell the truth. Didn't you see that he was trying to trap us?'

'We can't explore the channels here any more,' he said.

'No, but we could go to Memmert,' I said.

'There's nothing at Memmert,' said Davies, 'or von Brüning wouldn't have told us so much about it.'

'Well, we've got to go to Norderney . . .' I began, but Davies interrupted me.

'And *why* did you have to talk about Fräulein Dollmann?'

At last we had reached the heart of the matter.

'You haven't been fair with me, have you?' I asked. 'There's something about her you haven't told me.'

'I know I haven't,' said Davies quietly.

'Well, you see, I *had* to talk about her, for two reasons. First, you seemed very embarrassed when we were talking about the Dollmanns. And second, although you described Dollmann's short cut very well, in the way we had agreed, it was still obvious that he had treated you badly. So why would you still feel friendly towards him? Why would you want to see him again? Your – your feeling for *her* explains everything, you see – why

46

you were embarrassed, and why you want to see the Dollmanns again.'

'I find it very difficult to talk about things like this,' said Davies, without looking at me. 'I should have told you before, but I couldn't. The truth is, I do like – Clara, very much. And I think she likes me too.' Our eyes met for a second, in which all was said that needed to be said. 'But I'm sure she knows nothing about what her father's doing,' he continued. 'I'm sure she's got nothing to do with it. And I hoped we could avoid bringing her into it.'

'Are you really sure?' I asked. 'Don't you think she could be part of it? After all, you told me she encouraged you to follow them to Cuxhaven.'

'Carruthers,' said Davies seriously, 'I realize you're trying to help, but I know she's completely innocent. I just know it. We mustn't involve her.'

'Very well,' I replied. 'In that case, the best thing we can do is to forget the whole thing, and sail for England tonight.'

'No!' cried Davies. 'We can't do that. My God! We can't let Dollmann carry on. He's a traitor, working for the Germans, against his own country!'

'All right,' I said. 'I agree with you. We must go on with it. But we can't do so without involving her.'

'Are you quite sure we can't?' he asked.

'Of course we can't,' I replied. 'We've got to see him again. We've got to see both of them, in fact. And we must be friendly. You must tell the story you told today, and hope he believes it. Even if he doesn't, he won't dare say so, and we still have chances. And we must be friendly with them *both*.'

Davies said nothing, but his face showed great pain. In the

time we had been together, I had come to know Davies very well, and to understand how his honest mind worked. His strongest feeling was a deep love for his country, and a wish to serve her in any way he could. Now he had been given an unexpected chance to do something really important for his country, something that only he could do. But, at the same time, he loved Clara Dollmann, the daughter of a suspected traitor. It seemed that he could not take his great chance without hurting the woman he loved. It was a terrible position to be in.

'Are you sure you wouldn't rather leave it and sail for England tonight?' I asked gently.

Davies didn't hesitate. 'We can't do that. Perhaps there's some way we can stop Dollmann without involving her. If not, it can't be helped. We must go on with it.'

We discussed Memmert for some time. I felt sure that the search for the *Corinne*'s gold was a way of hiding what was really happening on Memmert, but Davies disagreed. He still felt that the channels through the sands held the answer to the riddle. In the end, we decided that we would sail next day to Norderney, and we would make the next plan when we got there.

6

A young lady and a book

We left Bensersiel the next morning, but the wind had dropped, just when we needed it most, and sometimes we did not seem to be moving at all, but were just rolling from side to side. In the distance we saw the *Blitz*, travelling rapidly westwards, and I felt sure the *Kormoran* would also be on her way to Norderney.

I was desperately impatient to get on, but it took us most of the day to reach Langeoog, and we anchored that night near Baltrum, in a thick white fog. The next morning we continued our painfully slow journey, and in the afternoon I heard Davies shout at last, 'There's Norderney!' I looked up and saw, through the mist, a group of grassy sandhills, exactly like a hundred others I had seen recently, but of much greater interest to me.

I was busy with the lead line, as we were in shallow water, when Davies suddenly said, 'Is that a boat ahead?'

'The *Kormoran*, do you think?' I asked, noticing what looked like a fishing boat in the distance.

Davies said nothing, and seemed to forget that he was steering the boat. We touched the sandbank, but luckily the tide pushed us away again. His next words surprised me. 'Let go the anchor. Lower the sail.'

When I had done this, Davies was still staring into the mist through his binoculars, and, to my astonishment, I noticed that his hands were trembling violently. I had never seen this happen before, even at moments of great danger.

'What's the matter?' I asked. 'Are you cold?'

'That little boat,' he said. 'It's her, I'm sure. It's the *Medusa*'s dinghy. She's come to meet m—, I mean, us.' He pushed the binoculars into my hand, and I saw a pretty little white sail coming closer. I kept my eyes on the boat, as I did not want to look at Davies. At last I heard him draw a deep breath. He turned to the *Dulcibella*'s dinghy.

'You come, too,' he offered, jumping in and picking up the oars.

'I'd rather stay. I'll tidy up the cabin.'

'Carruthers,' said Davies, 'if she comes aboard, please remember she's outside this business. There are no clues to be got from her.'

'I'll keep out of it this time,' I said. 'You do and say what you like.'

He rowed away, just as he was, with unbrushed hair and in his old sailing clothes. I watched the two boats getting closer in the mist, and heard a great splashing of oars. Finally I saw the boats being pulled up on a sandbank, and then two figures walking rapidly to meet each other. And then I thought it was time to go below to tidy the cabin.

Nothing on earth could have made the *Dulcibella*'s cabin a suitable place to receive a lady, but I did my best, putting clothes away in cupboards, a clean cloth on the table, and books back on the shelf. I had just put water on to boil for tea, when I heard the dinghy return.

I went up on deck, and found Davies with a very pretty girl, about nineteen years old. She was wearing a thick jacket, dark skirt and rubber boots, and her rose-brown skin lent a delicious touch of colour to the greyness of the sea and sky. When she looked at me and spoke, I knew immediately that she was no

'Fräulein Dollmann', but as English as I was, although she must have spoken German ever since she was a child.

She looked eagerly round the yacht, asking questions about all she saw, but it was obvious that she was more interested in Davies himself. The way she looked at him, and the way he looked at her, made me feel sorry for myself, because I was not in love, and even sorrier for Davies, because I could not see how all this would end. One thing was clear, however. She could never have been involved in her father's attempt to kill Davies.

'How *did* you manage alone that day?' she asked him suddenly. 'You know, on the way to Cuxhaven.'

'Oh, it was quite safe,' replied Davies. 'But it's much better to have a friend.'

She looked at me, and – well, I was suddenly extremely proud to be Davies's friend.

'Father said you'd be safe,' she said.

We went below into the cabin, where the water was just beginning to boil. Miss Dollmann was in a light-hearted mood, laughing and joking about all our little domestic arrangements.

'You will stop at Norderney?' she asked us.

I looked at Davies. It was up to him. But I need not have doubted him. There was no hesitation in his reply. 'Yes, of course we shall. I'd like to see your father again.'

'Ye–es,' she said, anxiously, 'yes, I'm sure he will be glad to see you.' She did not sound at all certain. 'He'll be back tomorrow. You know, we aren't living on the *Medusa* at the moment, but in our house on Norderney. My stepmother is there too.' She gave Davies the address, a little unwillingly, it seemed to me.

The difficult moment passed and a warm and friendly feeling returned to the cabin as the three of us sat down to enjoy our tea

51

together. But that pleasant event never took place – all because of an English name in gold-painted letters on the cover of an old book on our bookshelf. The disaster came and went so quickly that at the time I had no idea what caused it. One moment our visitor was laughing and talking to Davies, while looking through some of our books. Then suddenly there was an awful silence, and I turned round from making the tea. She was sitting quite still, with eyes wide open, and a very white, frightened face.

After a few seconds, she managed to speak. 'How late it is – I really must go. My boat won't be safe.' She got up from the table.

'What's the matter?' asked Davies in English, but she did not answer, and almost ran up the ladder, like a wounded animal trying to escape. She had reached the deck and jumped into the dinghy, before she realized she needed one of us to go with her and bring the boat back.

'Davies can . . .' I began, but she interrupted me.

'Oh, no, thank you. If you will be so kind, Herr Carruthers. It's your turn. I mean—'

'Go on,' said Davies to me in English. I jumped into the dinghy. The poor girl tried to apologize to Davies, but could not find the right words.

'Goodbye,' he said simply, and turned away.

I offered to row, but she took no notice and rowed fast towards her sailing boat. It was now floating gently off the sandbank, where it was anchored.

'Herr Carruthers,' she said. 'I want to say something to you.' (It sounded like von Brüning's warning all over again.) 'I made a mistake just now. It's not a good idea for you to call on us at Norderney tomorrow. My father is always busy.'

'We can come another day. We have several days to spare,'

Clara was sitting quite still, with eyes wide open,
and a very white, frightened face.

I said, 'and we have to stop at Norderney for letters, anyway.'

'Please don't come because of us,' she said. 'This fine weather may not last. It would be a pity not to use it to sail to England. And my father will be too busy to see you, I know.'

'But we could see *you*, surely,' I replied.

'No, no, please,' she said quickly. 'My father would not like it. I should not have come today. Please tell Herr Davies that – he must not come near us.'

'He'll understand,' I said. 'I know he'll be very sorry, but you can always trust him to do the right thing.'

'Yes, I know I can,' she said softly. 'Goodbye. Please say goodbye to Herr Davies for me.'

✧   ✧   ✧

I rowed back to the yacht, where I found Davies in the cabin. He had taken down all the books from the shelf, and was staring at the one he held in his hand.

'What on earth can have upset her?' I asked.

'I've just realized,' he said. 'It was this,' and he handed me the book. I had seen it before on the shelf, but never opened it. It was about sailing on the east coast of England, with all the usual details of winds and tides.

'What about it?' I asked, puzzled.

'Don't you see? She was looking at this book,' said Davies. 'Look at the photograph at the front.'

I looked. It showed a young man on the deck of a small yacht. 'Well?' I still could not understand.

'It's him!'

'Who?'

'Dollmann!' cried Davies. 'Dollmann wrote it! She was upset because now we know who her father really is!'

I looked at the front of the book. The author was Captain X of the Royal Navy. The book had been written sixteen years before. 'Are you sure it's him?' I asked.

'Quite sure,' Davies replied. He looked again at the picture. 'Yes, that's Dollmann, all right.'

'So, sixteen years ago he was an officer in the British Navy, and now he's working for the Germans,' I said slowly. 'He's about fifty now, you said, so that fits in. And the girl has been speaking German since she was a child. They must have come to Germany soon after he wrote the book. Is it a well-known book?'

'I've never seen another copy,' said Davies. 'I bought this one for a few pence, in a second-hand bookshop.'

'Didn't you say that Dollmann visited you on the *Dulcibella* in September?' I asked.

'Of course! He must have seen the book. Perhaps he thought I'd recognized him. That explains everything!'

'Does it?' I said. 'Perhaps he's just someone who did something wrong, had to leave the navy, and came here, where nobody knew him, to start a new life.'

'No, that's not it,' said Davies. 'That doesn't explain why Grimm's been watching us, or why von Brüning suspects us. What do you think of the daughter?' he added.

'She's lovely, Davies,' I said. 'You'll be a lucky man if . . . well, better not think about that for the moment. I'm sorry I ever thought badly of her. I can see she's quite innocent of any unpleasant business. Mind you, she's aware that they have a past to hide. This makes the problem much more difficult for us, doesn't it?'

'Not at all,' said Davies. 'It just means that there are two things we must do. We must find out exactly what Dollmann is doing and stop him, and we've got to make sure *she* doesn't suffer because of *his* guilt.'

'He's still away,' I said.

'Yes, I know. But she said he's coming back on the ferry from the mainland tomorrow morning. We'd better be there when he arrives.'

We arrived at Norderney town in the evening, and anchored on the edge of the deep water channel, about fifty metres from the harbour entrance. We were too excited to sleep, or do anything except make plans, and talk. At last Davies's natural shyness left him, and I was able to see into the secret corners of his heart. He loved this girl, and he loved his country, and he was determined to be loyal to both of them. Somehow, a way must be found to do this.

After much discussion, we realized there was only one answer – to get Dollmann, secrets and all, daughter and all, away from Germany completely. This was now our goal, and we took delight in the challenge. We had no clear idea how we would reach the goal, but there were two possible ways forward. One was to continue searching the area for clues of some kind; and the other was to use this new information about Dollmann to force him to tell us what was going on. By the time we went to bed, this second plan was the preferred one.

A day out in the fog

When the ferry from the mainland arrived the next morning, we were watching it from the *Dulcibella*'s cabin.

'That's Dollmann,' said Davies, ' the tall one with the beard.'

'Who's that with him?' I asked. It was a short, fat, older man, with glasses and a hard-looking, clever face.

'He must be the engineer from Bremen, who von Brüning told us about. Look, there's Grimm, behind him.'

Five or six passengers got off the ferry, but Dollmann and his companions stayed on the deck. They stared down at the *Dulcibella* as the ferry moved out of the harbour.

'They haven't got off!' I said. 'Where are they going?'

'Juist,' Davies answered. 'It's the only other stop.'

'And from Juist to Memmert,' I said softly.

We had to go into Norderney town to buy food and milk, and to collect my post. I was surprised to find that there were two letters for me from my boss. The first one gave me permission to take another week's holiday. The second one, written two days later, and marked 'Urgent', cancelled this permission, and told me to return as arranged. I showed them to Davies.

'I haven't received this second one,' I said with a smile.

As we made our way back to the harbour, a thick curtain of fog rolled in from the sea. 'We'll never find the yacht in this fog,' I said, as we climbed down to the dinghy.

'Yes, we will,' said Davies. 'Just row straight across the harbour.' He leaned over the side of the boat, feeling in the water with a stick. 'There we are,' he said, after a few moments. 'That's the edge of the deep water channel. Now all we've got to do is follow it until we reach the *Dulcibella*. It couldn't be simpler.' And, sure enough, in two or three minutes we were back on the yacht.

'That's extraordinary,' I said. 'How far could you go like that?'

'Well,' he replied. 'If we had a chart and a compass, I suppose we could go anywhere.'

'*Why not go to Memmert?*' I said quietly.

'Memmert!' he said. 'That's an idea! It's a long way, of course, twenty kilometres, more or less.'

'Yes,' I said eagerly. 'But what a chance! Everyone's seen the *Dulcibella* here, including Dollmann and his friends. If we could get to Memmert in this fog, we might find out what's going on. And no one would see us on the way, or know we were there.'

Davies took down the chart and studied it. 'Put some food and water in the dinghy,' he said. 'And an oil lamp, the compass and the guns.'

'The guns?' I said. 'What for?'

'We're looking for ducks, if the fog clears,' he smiled. 'Now, just give me ten minutes with the chart.'

I had got the boat ready by the time he joined me. 'We'll have to hurry,' he said. 'We can't take the open sea route, round Juist. It's too public – that's the way the ferry goes. And it's more than twenty-five kilometres. No, we'll have to go over the sand. It's a much shorter way, but it'll be difficult because the tide's falling, so the channels through the sandbanks will be extremely narrow and shallow. Are you sure you can row there and back?'

'You steer, and I'll row all right,' I said. And we set out.

Even at high tide, the chart only shows narrow channels between Norderney and Memmert, and in a little over three hours' time, it would be low tide. The fog made the sandbanks completely invisible, but Davies did not attempt to look around for buoys or marker posts. Instead, he concentrated all his attention on the chart, the compass, and his watch. My duty was to be a machine, to keep the dinghy moving in whatever direction he wanted. I pulled hard, breathing deeply and regularly, hoping I would be fit enough to manage the journey.

At the shallowest point, Davies dropped the lead line into the water, and measured the depth. My oar touched sand, and we were aground. I rested for a moment, while Davies looked at his chart. Then we were off again, with a push from the oars on the sandbank, and I could see from Davies's shining eyes that we were in the right channel.

We continued in this way, rowing and pushing, through the soundless white blanket of fog. I began to lose all idea of time and place. The misty figure of Davies in front of me seemed as dream-like and crazy as myself, and I saw strange, imaginary shapes appearing out of nowhere.

It was a race against time, the fog, and the falling tide, but in the early afternoon we arrived at Memmert. In four and a half hours I had rowed twenty kilometres, and Davies had steered us through fog and sandbanks without a single mistake. I let my tired muscles relax, and we had some whisky, bread and cold meat, while making our plans. We decided Davies would stay with the boat, while I explored. I spoke the language well, and in my sea-boots, sailing clothes, and old hat, I could easily pass for a Frisian Islander in the fog.

'Take the compass, the chart, and the whistle,' said Davies.

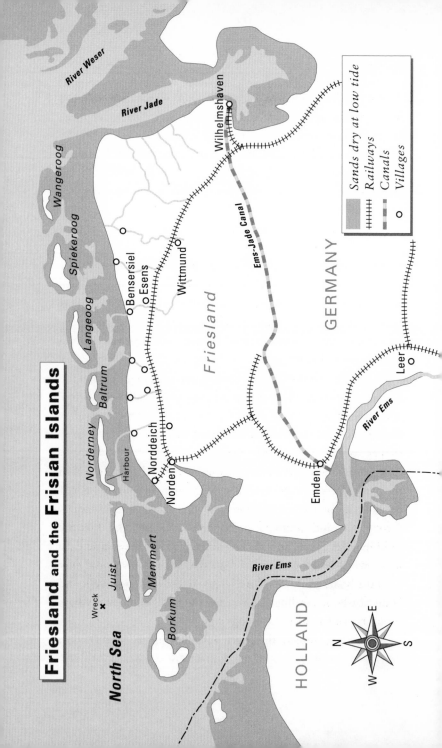

'Remember the tide – you can have an hour and a half, no more. If you can't find your way back, blow your whistle, and I'll blow mine to guide you. Good luck.'

The chart showed that the office building was north-west of where we had landed. 'That means south-east to come back,' I said to myself. I checked the compass, and started up the beach.

I could only see a few metres ahead of me in the fog, but I could hear noises all around me – a ship's bell, and some men calling to each other in German. Somewhere in front a door banged. Before long, I found myself on a path, and a few moments later a wall appeared, which seemed to be the side of a building. I paused, and took out my pipe and lit it, to give myself an excuse for standing still and listening.

I could hear a number of men's voices, so I moved away from the sound, round the corner of the building, and saw a lighted window ahead of me. It would be interesting to see into that room, I thought, so with my hat pulled well down, I walked slowly on, taking a long careful look inside as I passed. It seemed to be an office. I could see Grimm paying a workman some money, and in chairs round the room I could see von Brüning and Dollmann, and the short, older man from the ferry (who was, we learnt later, the Bremen engineer, Böhme). The room was brightly lit and no one was looking out through the window, so I went back for a closer inspection. Bending low, I moved, as quietly as a cat, until I was beneath the window. Then, with great care, I raised my head.

There was a different workman in the room now, also receiving his wages from Grimm. There were charts on the wall, and the plan of a ship. On the floor were several pieces of old wood, perhaps from the wreck itself. My heart sank. This was pay-day, with the boat crews and divers getting their wages – just an ordinary meeting of the directors of the company. Davies and I had come all this way for nothing!

I nearly turned and walked away at that point, but the faint voice of reason told me to be patient. 'There are your four men,' the voice said. 'Wait.'

Two more men came in to get their wages, and left. Then Grimm stood up and came over to the window. I quickly bent down low, and heard above me the curtains being pulled shut. There was the sound of chairs moving, and people sitting down. Another meeting seemed to be beginning.

Desperate to hear what they were saying, I put my ear as close to the window as possible, but I could only hear a few words now and then. First Dollmann spoke for several minutes. He seemed to be talking about a recent visit to England, and I heard the word 'Chatham'. Next, Böhme went through a report. He used the letters A to G; seven letters, with figures added to each of them, like this: 'A . . . bad . . . one point five; B . . . three weeks . . . thirty; C . . . thirty-two . . . one point two.' And so on. Then he asked Grimm about each of these seven letters. I could only hear odd words of Grimm's answers: 'tugs', 'railway', 'pilots', 'depth of water', and the name 'Esens'.

Suddenly I heard Böhme ask about 'the two Englishmen'. They were talking about Davies and myself. It seemed that Böhme wanted to meet us.

'Very well, sir,' Dollmann said, more loudly than before. 'I'll invite them to dinner this evening. You can see them then.'

We would have to get back to the yacht as quickly as possible. I was just about to move, when I heard movement inside the room. Two of the men pushed back their chairs and stood up, and I heard the door open and close. Who had left, and who remained? I waited, my ear hard against the window.

'He insists on coming,' said Böhme.

'Ach!' said von Brüning, sounding astonished.

'I said on the 25th. The tide will be right. He'll come on the night train, of course. Tell Grimm to be ready.'

There was a question from von Brüning.

'Only one, with half a load,' replied Böhme. 'How's the fog?' he added.

I slid away from the window before von Brüning pulled back the curtain. I looked at my watch – I had been away nearly an hour and a half. I had to get back to the boat, so I checked the compass and started walking. As soon as I was about a hundred metres from the building, I began to run. When I reached the shore, the tide was coming in fast but there was no sign of Davies or the dinghy. I had no time to go looking for them, so I blew my whistle. Almost immediately I heard another whistle some way off, *behind* me. I turned and ran towards it, blowing my whistle again. The other whistle answered and, a few moments later, I saw the dinghy.

'Quick, Davies,' I called softly. 'We must get back. Dollmann's going to invite us to dinner this evening.'

'Right,' said Davies. 'The tide's coming in, and the sands will be covered. We can take the direct route back to Norderney over the sandbanks.'

We both rowed and, with the rising tide to help us, we covered the distance in about three hours. Soon after we left, a wind began to blow from the west, and the fog rolled away as quickly as it had come. We were almost at Norderney when we saw behind us the lights of a motorboat. Davies guessed it was the

Blitz's launch, and we watched it draw level and pass us, going in the direction of Norderney.

'Now they'll know what we've been doing!' I cried.

'No, it's too dark now for them to recognize us,' said Davies. 'Let's slow down a bit. We don't want them to see us arrive looking all hot and exhausted. We'll have to pretend we just went out for a row. Will you be able to talk to them? My German's not good enough for that.'

'No, but I'll have to make the effort. If they suspect us now, we're finished.'

'Give me your oar, old man, and put your jacket on.' He lit his pipe, and rowed slowly on, while I lay back, trying to separate my mind from my exhausted body.

When we arrived, the launch was anchored beside the *Dulcibella*, but we could only see two of von Brüning's men on deck. Then we saw von Brüning himself appear from the *Dulcibella*'s cabin.

'Is that you, Herr Davies?' he said. 'We came to see you!'

Then someone else came up the ladder from the cabin, and Dollmann appeared. Davies sat quietly in the dinghy, looking up at his enemy, while Dollmann stared down at him from the deck of the *Dulcibella*. It was fortunate that Davies's expression was hidden in the darkness, but the lights from the launch fell pitilessly on Dollmann's smiling face, and showed me the thin lips and cold eyes of the man who had tried to drown my friend.

Meanwhile, the third of our uninvited guests, Herr Böhme, had reached the top of the ladder. There they stood, the three of them, like guilty schoolboys caught stealing apples, while we, the true offenders, only had to listen to their explanations. Dollmann explained he had seen the yacht in the harbour, and

Davies sat quietly in the dinghy, while Dollmann stared down at him from the deck of the Dulcibella.

had called on his return from Memmert to ask us to dinner at his house. Finding no one on board, he had meant to leave a note for Davies in the cabin. 'My friend, Herr Böhme, was eager to see round the yacht, and I knew you would not mind,' he added.

'Not at all,' said Davies pleasantly. 'And we'll come to dinner with pleasure. But we must change clothes first.'

'Where have you been?' asked von Brüning, smiling.

'Oh, rowing about since the fog cleared,' said Davies.

'Looking for ducks again,' I added, lifting my gun.

'No luck, I suppose?' laughed von Brüning. 'Come, my friends, we must leave these young sportsmen to get changed, and talk to them later.'

And with some embarrassment, the three men stepped on to the launch, which moved smoothly away. We went straight down to the cabin to see what they had been looking at. Everything was just as we had left it, except Dollmann's book, which was pushed right to the back of the shelf.

'Aha!' I said, showing it to Davies. 'I think this proves Dollmann has something to hide from *them*.'

'Yes,' said Davies. 'It shows that they know his real name – or why would he try to hide the book from them? But they probably don't know he wrote a book, and that I have a copy.'

'It's quite complicated, wondering who knows what,' I said. 'Dollmann can't be sure what *we* know, and must be terrified of the others finding out that we know who he is – if we do. It's becoming clear, though, that they don't trust him.'

I had told Davies what I had heard and seen on Memmert as we rowed back. Now, as we quickly washed, and changed our clothes, we went over it again.

'What are there seven of in this area?' I asked.

'Islands, of course,' replied Davies.

'Yes, but what about "railway" and "Esens"?' I said. 'And someone insists on coming, on the night train, on the 25th. It must be someone important. Böhme, von Brüning, and Grimm are going to meet him. Somewhere at high tide, probably. And Dollmann probably doesn't know about it as they didn't discuss it until he was out of the room.'

Davies thought for a moment. 'Well, it could be Norddeich. There's a station there, and, let's see . . . high tide will be somewhere between ten-thirty and eleven o'clock on the 25th. What shall we do?'

'Look,' I said, 'we want a fresh start. We need to find out a lot more, and we need to prove to them that we're harmless. I suggest that I go back to London.'

'To London!' cried Davies, looking shocked.

'I can find out about Dollmann's past there, and then come back here, as somebody else, to follow up the clues on the 25th. Meanwhile, you must stay here, pretend you want to do a little duck shooting, that sort of thing.'

'I'll be no good alone,' he said miserably. 'I really don't like the idea, but I trust your judgement.'

'We haven't got time to think about it now, or we'll be late for dinner. I think they want to inspect us, or at least, Böhme does, and he's obviously the important one.'

'What are we going to say?' demanded Davies, in a worried voice.

'Not a word about where we've been today,' I said. 'If they discover that, we'll be in trouble, and in prison too, probably. For the rest, tell the truth. It's all we can do.'

8

An evening with the enemy

When we arrived at the house, a servant showed us into the living-room, where a hot wave of perfume and cigarette smoke hit us. The room was richly furnished and overheated, very different from our living conditions on the *Dulcibella*. Von Brüning, looking relaxed as usual, was talking to Clara on a sofa, while Dollmann rose from an armchair to greet us, and Böhme appeared from a doorway. Dollmann welcomed us politely enough, but his intelligent eyes did not leave us for a moment, and there was a certain falseness in his manner. He introduced me to his wife, Clara's stepmother. She was a large, handsome woman, with unnaturally dark hair and red lips, wearing a low-cut evening dress. I may add that she was unmistakeably German. It was clear that her main concern was to encourage von Brüning and Clara to take an interest in each other.

Clara was trying to avoid looking at us. I hoped she hadn't told her father about her visit to us on the yacht. She was doing her best to appear normal, but at times I caught an expression of deep misery on her lovely face.

'Well, are we never going to have dinner?' cried Frau Dollmann impatiently, and we all moved into the dining-room, where we sat down around a large table. I was beginning to feel the effects of my long day's rowing, and the heat and my anxiety made me feel quite faint. But a glass of wine and some excellent food soon concentrated my mind on the dangers of our situation.

'I'm leaving Davies, you know,' I said lightly, to the whole table. 'Life on the *Dulcibella* is too hard for a lazy weekend sailor like me.'

There was silence, until von Brüning said, 'Why are you going so suddenly, Herr Carruthers?'

'Oh, didn't I tell you I had to call at the post office for letters? I received two from my boss, and he wants me back in London at once, unfortunately.'

Another uncomfortable silence was broken by Dollmann, who turned to Davies and began, 'By the way, I ought to apologize to you for—'

This was something I did not want to appear involved in, so I said to Frau Dollmann, 'How awful the fog was today!'

'Have you been in the harbour all day?' she asked.

'Oh yes. We couldn't leave the yacht alone in the fog,' I replied, with professional seriousness.

Von Brüning joined in with a laugh. 'I don't think that's *your* opinion! You are much too fond of dry land!'

Meanwhile, I could hear Davies and Dollmann discussing the Hohenhörn – 'my fault' and 'quite safe', I heard my friend say. Suddenly Böhme, who had been looking closely at them both, turned and said to me, 'So, when are you setting out for England? Tomorrow?'

'Yes. There's a ferry at 8.15 in the morning, I think.'

'Good. We shall be companions. I'm going to Bremen, so we'll travel as far as Leer together. How pleasant!'

'Very,' I agreed. 'Is this only a short stay for you?'

'The same as usual. I visit the work at Memmert once a month, and spend a night or two here.'

I decided to play a dangerous game. 'Memmert,' I said, 'now do tell me more about Memmert. Von Brüning told us a little, but it all seems so secret! For example, all three of you had one of your mysterious meetings on Memmert today. You'd just come from there when you came to visit the *Dulcibella*. Why today? Was something important happening there? Were you inspecting the gold? No, *I* know! You were taking it to the mainland!'

'*I* can't help you,' smiled Böhme. 'I'm only the company engineer. Ask von Brüning for help.'

I turned to the commander. 'My dear young detective,' he laughed, 'I'm not very closely involved in all this. Try the company director. Rescue me, Herr Dollmann!'

'I,' said Dollmann, with a noisy laugh, 'cannot tell company secrets. Business interests must be protected!'

'Well,' I said, 'I wonder – Do you remember, Davies, how interested the commander was in all our doings, when we met at Bensersiel? I wonder if he feared that our explorations might possibly lead us to Memmert?'

'Really,' said von Brüning, with a smile, 'I thought I was being most helpful to you, giving advice about duck shooting and so on. But go on, young man.'

'What is he talking about, and why go on with this stupid mystery?' asked Dollmann's wife, yawning.

Why indeed? My head was turning as I thought desperately fast. If I went too far in this direction, they might guess the truth, but if I didn't go far enough, they might also suspect us. 'I was thinking about this delightful dinner party,' I continued, 'and the reason for it. Now I think I can guess why you invited us. Didn't you discuss us at Memmert? And didn't one of you, perhaps Herr Böhme, who hadn't met either of us, suggest an invitation?'

'You could almost have *been* there,' said Dollmann.

'You may thank your terrible climate that we weren't,' I replied, laughing. 'I also think – but, no – this is going too far. I shall probably offend you.'

'Come, let's hear it. Your wild ideas are amusing.'

'Well, you know, we were a little surprised to find you *all* on board the *Dulcibella*, taking such a deep interest in a small boat! I think you wanted to *inspect* us!'

Everybody burst out laughing, and Dollmann said, 'I warned you, Böhme. We really must apologize.'

'The point is, what did you suspect me of?' I went on. 'I know you can't suspect Davies – just look at him!'

'Perhaps we *still* suspect you,' said von Brüning.

'Oho! You'll force me to take action. Perhaps when I get back to London, I'll do some investigating! There must be some questions to ask about the ownership of the *Corinne*'s gold.'

There was another silence, finally broken by Dollmann, who turned to Böhme and von Brüning and said, half-jokingly, 'Gentlemen, we must come to an agreement with this dangerous young man. What can we offer Herr Carruthers?'

'Take me to Memmert!' I said. 'Then I'll forgive you.'

'But you are starting for England tomorrow!'

'I ought to, but I'll stay for that.'

'Under promise of absolute secrecy, then?' said Böhme.

'And you'll show me everything? Wreck and all?'

'Everything, if you can put on a diving suit and dive.'

'We've won!' I cried delightedly. 'And now, I don't mind saying that the joke's at an end, as far as I'm concerned. In spite of your kind offer, I must start for England tomorrow. You see, I really did receive letters from my boss. Do you want to see them?' I pulled the letters from my pocket, and gave them to

Dollmann. 'Ah, you don't read English easily, perhaps. I expect Herr Böhme does.'

The dinner continued, with more food and even more wine. I drank as little as possible, to keep my head clear. I knew that our enemies had allowed me to win the first part of the game, but I felt sure they knew more about us than they appeared to. However, I guessed we would probably be safe, as long as they believed we thought Memmert, and Memmert only, was the centre of their secret activities. I also knew that they could not suspect us of having been to Memmert that day, because nobody would believe it was possible to do what Davies and I had done.

I have no way of knowing how near we came to being arrested that night, but once or twice we must have been very close. There could not have been a more interesting party of seven people anywhere in Europe that evening, with such differing feelings of fear, love, anger, ambition, and unhappiness, all hidden behind smiling faces.

We stayed for two hours or more, but soon the cigarette smoke and heat brought back my faintness, and my tired arms and legs began to stiffen. We rose to go, and although I do not remember much about the goodbyes, I heard Böhme say he would see me on the ferry the next day. Von Brüning was staying at the house a little longer.

'You want to be able to talk about us!' I remember saying, with a last effort at cheerfulness.

Outside in the fresh air, it was a silver, breathless night. And back on the yacht, I fell on to one of the benches, fully dressed. There I slept such a deep sleep that von Brüning's men could have tied me up and taken me to prison, without my noticing a thing.

9

The answer to the riddle

'Goodbye, old man,' called Davies, as the ferry pulled slowly out of Norderney. He looked tired and depressed as he waved goodbye to me, and I was only half awake myself. It was Davies who had woken me, fed me, and packed my bag with motherly care. We had not had time to discuss any further plans, except that he should expect my return on about the 26th, the day after the Germans' meeting.

Böhme was on the ferry too, keeping a close eye on me. However, I managed to get away from him for a few minutes, in order to read Davies's note to me, which he had put into my hand at the last moment. It said:

Their meeting: could be at Norden. It has a station, and high tide there on the 25th will be 10.30 to 11 p.m. Can't be Norddeich, because it has a deep channel for the ferry, so no need to worry about the tide being right.

Other clues: tugs, pilots, depths, railway, Esens, seven of something – could this mean a land-and-sea defence plan for the North Sea coast?

Sea: there are seven islands from Borkum to Wangeroog (not counting Memmert, which is small), each with its own channel to the mainland. Tugs and pilots needed for finding these channels.

Land: good railway line running only a few kilometres from the coast, connecting inland villages. Is Esens the centre of this defence plan?

But I was too sleepy to concentrate fully, and I slept for most of the train journey that followed our arrival at Norddeich, only waking up twice. The first time was at Emden, where Böhme and I had to change trains, and I heard someone talking to him about canals. The second was at Leer station, when Böhme woke me to say goodbye. 'Don't forget to do your investigating in London!' he cried, smiling falsely.

As the day passed, however, I began to feel fresher, and was able to think more clearly. Today was the 23rd, so I had very little time to reach London, find out about Dollmann, and return in time for the meeting on the 25th. I began to imagine how it would be in London – trying to persuade people in government offices of the urgency of my enquiries. Oh, will you leave a note, sir? Or come back next week to see Mr So-and-So? People are cautious, unwilling to give out information unless they are forced to. And the Navy!

Another thought. How sure was I of Davies's safety while I was away? Might they offer to take him to Memmert, put him in a diving-suit, cut off the air – Stop, that was nonsense! But I had already decided there was no point in returning to London. Instead, I would go as far as Amsterdam, to change my clothes and identity, and sleep just one night in a comfortable bed. Then I would go back to Friesland to look for more clues, and try to solve the riddle.

In Amsterdam, I sent this telegram to my boss:

Very sorry, could not call Norderney for post. Hope extra holiday all right. Please write Hotel du Louvre, Paris.

I found a pleasant hotel, and slept for ten hours in a huge, luxurious bed. Early next morning, I was on a train travelling back the way I had come, wearing some old seaman's clothes, which I had bought from a second-hand clothes shop. I was now an ordinary English seaman, going to Emden to join his ship.

All day, as I was carried through the Dutch and German countryside, I puzzled over the clues we had gathered. Davies was probably right, and Norden was the place for the meeting on the 25th. 'The tide will be right,' they had said at Memmert, and high tide was between 10.30 and 11 p.m. My train timetable told me there was a 'night train', too, leaving at 7.43 p.m, and stopping at all the villages east of Norden. I determined to be at Norden in time for the meeting, and until then, I would find out all I could about Friesland, and Esens in particular.

At Emden, I bought a ticket to Esens. The train crossed a big canal, which I realized was the Ems–Jade Canal, connecting Emden and Wilhelmshaven, and deep enough to carry gunboats. I looked again at my map of the area. Esens was six kilometres inland from Bensersiel, and a stream ran all the way from Bensersiel to join the Esens–Wittmund Canal. I suddenly remembered the numbers I had heard at Memmert. Perhaps they were the depths of water in canals! The conversation I had heard at Emden station also came back to me, and I felt sure that Böhme was a *canal* engineer. Was I getting somewhere at last?

In Esens, I walked around in the evening light and discovered several interesting things. A lot of work was being done there, on developing the Bensersiel stream into a canal. I also saw a long, low building, rather like buildings I had seen on Memmert, where barges were being built. I climbed into one of the barges to inspect it more closely, and realized that it was designed not only for canal work, but also for rough water.

By now it was midnight, and as there was no one around, I decided to spend the night on the barge. The cold wooden boards brought back the memory of my soft hotel bed, but a spy can't expect luxury every night. At least there was more room to move than on the *Dulcibella*.

The next day was the 25th. In the morning I studied the map again and realized how much I had to explore. There were six more villages like Esens and six more harbours like Bensersiel round the coast, and perhaps these matched Böhme's seven letters, A to G. All seven harbours had channels going through the sands to the open sea, and all seven were connected by a stream or canal to an inland village.

I spent the whole day walking round Friesland. This time I took the identity of a German seaman, and talked to local people, to find out more. I was only suspected of being English once, but that nearly got me into serious trouble. Luckily, however, I managed to get the man drunk and escape from him. But it made me more aware of the danger I was in, so after that I avoided roads and villages, and walked across fields and through streams. Everywhere I went, I discovered that work was going on; all the streams were close to becoming canals, and solid, good quality barges were being built in large numbers.

At 7.15 in the evening, I arrived, very tired, at Norden station, for the meeting I hoped would take place there. I was delighted to see von Brüning there already. He did not notice me in my dirty seaman's clothes, and I heard him ask for a ticket to Esens. I bought one, too, and we both got on the 7.43 train. At the last minute, I saw two late arrivals, whom I did not recognize, jump on. A whistle blew, and the train rolled slowly out of the station.

At Esens station, I got out first, and waited in the darkness for the three men to pass. They walked on together, away from the coast and towards the canal. I did not follow them, as I felt sure they would appear at Bensersiel very soon, so I walked quickly to the harbour. There I waited for an uneasy hour, looking at the barges lying at anchor, and wondering if I had guessed wrongly about their plans.

Suddenly I saw the lights of a tug coming into the small harbour. It was Grimm at the helm, with a crew of two seamen. He left them in charge while he jumped on to the shore, and disappeared in the direction of the canal.

I knew I had to get on board somehow – it was the only way I could follow them – but how? Fortunately for me, the sailors seemed very interested in the brightly lit pub, and after a short discussion, they tied up the tug, and hurried towards it. This was my chance, and I took it. As soon as they had gone, I ran across the mud, and climbed on board. The only place I could find to hide was the dinghy, which hung over the side of the tug, tied on with thick ropes. I was too excited to be anxious about what might happen if I was discovered, and I hid myself carefully at the bottom of the little boat.

Soon after, the sailors hurried back, followed by Grimm. The engine started, and the tug moved slowly away, and then stopped. I heard footsteps from the direction of the canal, and three people jumped on to the deck. We were off again, and this time the tug seemed to be pulling something. What was it? A barge, of course! I had seen one, half-loaded with bricks, lying near the tug in the harbour. (Then I remembered the words from Memmert: 'Only one, with half a load.')

Cautiously, I looked over the edge of the dinghy, and realized we were travelling west, towards Norderney, or Memmert, perhaps. I was perfectly safe, but *only until the dinghy was needed*. Grimm was steering, and the three passengers were standing at the back of the tug, watching the barge moving smoothly behind us. I recognized tall, bearded von Brüning, and short, fat Böhme, and the third man must be he who 'insists on coming'. I was almost sure I knew who he was.

Now the tug moved northwards, aiming for the channel between Langeoog and Baltrum. We were taking the open sea route, as the tide was falling, and it would be impossible to cross the sandbanks in the dark. Once through the channel, I expected us to turn west towards Norderney, but we carried on out to sea, where the water was a good deal rougher. After a while, the tug began to turn, and made one complete circle, though for what purpose I had no idea. The behaviour of the three passengers was also puzzling. They spent all the time watching, and clearly talking about, the barge behind us. Finally, we turned west again, in the direction of Memmert.

And then at last I understood. *This was the way to England too.* What I had just witnessed was a rehearsal for an invasion. This trial trip was designed to show how tugs could pull sea-going barges carrying soldiers and their weapons – hundreds of barges, carrying thousands of soldiers. This army would gather, not in some great naval harbour, but on an unimportant piece of coast, hidden behind the sandbanks of the Frisian Islands, where nobody would expect an invasion to start from. The barges would be brought down the canals to seven tiny harbours, and when the tide was right, the tugs would pull them through the channels that led between the islands to the open sea. And on to England – and its undefended east coast.

It was such a daring and clever plan that I found it difficult to believe. But I knew it must be true. Davies and I had never seriously considered that Dollmann and his friends had a plan

*The three passengers were standing at the back of the tug,
watching the barge moving smoothly behind us.*

of *attack*; we had only ever thought of it as *defensive* action. But bit by bit, the pieces of the puzzle fell into place, and I had solved the riddle at last.

I was still lost in these thoughts when the tug passed Norderney town and turned south. We were taking the narrow channel to Norddeich, where the passengers would probably land, and I would very likely be discovered in my hiding-place. Somehow I had to escape. Only a kilometre away was the *Dulcibella* and Davies, if he were safe. What would *he* do in this situation? The tide was falling, and we were crossing the sandbanks . . .

A wild idea came to me. I looked quickly at my watch, by the light of a match. It was 2.30 a.m. Low tide would be about 5 o'clock. The tug would be aground until about 7.30 a.m, not in any danger, but safely out of the way.

Grimm was below, in the cabin with his three passengers, while one of the crew was at the helm, with his back to me. Grimm and I were about the same height, and he had left his coat at the top of the ladder down to the cabin. I climbed very quietly out of the dinghy, put on his coat, and pulled my hat down to hide my face. Confidently I walked up to the helmsman, and touched him on the arm, as I had seen Grimm do earlier. The man, used to such commands from his silent captain, moved obediently away.

My plan developed beautifully. I took the helm, and kept the tug in the channel, between the buoys, until I felt the moment had come. Then I suddenly turned the wheel as hard as I could to the right. The seaman shouted a warning, but he was too late. The tug crashed into the sandbank at full speed, and the wheel went stiff in my hands. We were aground.

I think it is safe to say that I was the only one on board who behaved with calmness and common sense in the minutes that followed. Grimm was on deck in seconds, shouting angrily at his crew, and the passengers soon joined in. The wind, darkness and rain made the confusion worse. Unnoticed, I threw off Grimm's coat, and ran back to the dinghy. On the way, I bumped into the unknown passenger – 'he who insists'. He thought I was one of Grimm's men, and offered to help me. I saw his face close up, and realized immediately that my earlier suspicion was correct. The leader of the country can, after all, insist on what he likes.

The passenger and I cut the dinghy's ropes, and the boat hit the water with a loud splash. 'Lower the boat,' I heard Grimm shout, but we had already done it. I jumped in and took up the oars. The wind and tide caught me, and carried me rapidly northwards. I was very quickly out of sight of the barge, and began to row towards Norderney, with the tide. There was an outburst of shouting which soon died away. They would be held tight on the sandbank for at least five hours.

10

The last voyage

It was impossible to miss the way, and, helped by the wind and tide, I made short work of the journey. But where was the *Dulcibella*? Not where I had left her! I pulled feverishly into the harbour, and there – thank God! – I found her.

'Who's that?' came from below, as I stepped on board.

'Shh! It's me!'

We were both pleased to see each other again, and Davies asked anxiously, 'Are you all right, old man?'

'Yes, are you? Quick, a match! What's the time?'

'Ten past three. My God, Carruthers, what *have* you been doing?' I hadn't washed or shaved for two days, and must have looked quite wild.

'It's the invasion of England! Is Dollmann at the house?' I asked urgently.

'Invasion?' Davies repeated in astonishment.

'Is Dollmann at the house?'

'Yes, but what—'

'How soon can we leave harbour?' I interrupted.

'Ten minutes. First light is about five o'clock. Where are we going?'

'Holland, or England.'

'Are they invading it now?' said Davies calmly.

'No, only rehearsing,' I laughed, wildly. 'We have an hour and a half. We must go and tell Dollmann we know his secret, and get them both aboard. It's now or never!'

While Davies was dressing, I told him what I had discovered.
'Are you being watched?' I asked.

'I think so, by the men from the *Kormoran*. But they're not
here now. Grimm came and collected them in a tug.'

'Don't worry, they're all safely aground on the sands –
Grimm, Böhme, von Brüning, and "he who insists".'

Once more we hurried through the little town, walking on air,
I think; I remember no tiredness.

'I was right,' said Davies. 'The channels are the key to the
whole thing. We have no North Sea warships, no protection at
all for our coastline. They'd land on one of the quiet, deserted
sandy beaches on the east coast, far away from Chatham, our
only eastern naval port.'

'It seems rather a wild idea,' I remarked.

'Wild? So is *any* invasion. But it's planned in such detail! No
other country could organize it as well as that. I really think it
could succeed.'

We arrived at the house, and rang the door bell loudly. An
upstairs window opened, and I called up, 'A message from
Commander von Brüning – urgent.' The window closed, and
soon after, Dollmann opened the front door.

'Good morning, Captain X,' I said in English. 'Stop, we're
friends, you fool!' I added, as the door was nearly shut in our
faces. It opened slowly again, and we walked in.

'Silence!' he whispered. His hands were trembling, and his
face looked hot, but there was a smile – what a smile! – on his
lips. 'Well?' he said in English, when we were all in the living-
room.

'There's no time to lose,' I said. 'We sail for Holland, or
perhaps England, at five o'clock at the latest, and we want the

pleasure of your company. We promise you immunity, on certain conditions, which we'll discuss later. I'm afraid we only have room to take Miss Clara and yourself.'

His smile froze, and then suddenly he laughed. 'You fools,' he said. 'I thought I'd finished with you. My God, I'll give you five minutes to get away, or else I'll have you locked up as spies! What do you suspect me of?'

'You're a traitor, working for the Germans,' said Davies. We were both discouraged by this unexpected attack.

'A tra—? You stupid, crazy young fools! I'm in *British* service! You're destroying the work of years – and so close to success!'

For a second, Davies and I looked at each other in horror. He lied, he must be lying – but how could we make sure?

'Very well,' I said, after a moment, 'we'll leave, as it seems we've made a mistake – silence, Davies! – but we should tell you we know everything. I was taking notes at Memmert the other afternoon.'

'At Memmert? In the fog? Impossible!'

'Difficult, but not impossible. I heard you reporting on Chatham, and Böhme talking about the German A to G plan of defence. Of course, all that doesn't matter, now we know you're on the right side!'

'Not so loud!' Dollmann was lost in thought for a moment, and then said, 'I congratulate you, gentlemen, on your discoveries, but I shall have to have you arrested, or I myself may be suspected—'

'I'm sorry,' I interrupted, 'we're short of time. At Memmert I heard your friends make an appointment behind your back, and I took the trouble to attend the meeting. It was a rehearsal for the invasion of England. No, don't touch that gun. You see, you can arrest us if you like, but the secret's in safe hands. My London lawyer has the facts.'

'You lie!' He was right, but he could not know it. He fell into an armchair, and seemed to grow older and greyer as we watched.

'What did you say about immunity, and Clara?' he whispered.

'We're friends – we're friends!' burst out Davies, with a break in his voice. 'We want to help you both.' Through a sudden mist over my eyes, I saw him walk over and lay his hand on Dollmann's shoulder. 'Come with us. Wake her, tell her. It'll be too late soon.'

'Tell her? I can't tell her. *You* tell her, boy.' His shoulders were bent and his head was in his hands.

Davies turned to me. 'You go up, Carruthers,' he said.

'Look at me! I'll frighten her like this. *You* must.'

'Well, I – I don't like to.'

'Nonsense, man! We'll both go then.' We left Dollmann in his misery, and went quietly upstairs. A bedroom door was half open, and in the doorway stood a white figure.

'What is it, father?' she called in a whisper.

I pushed Davies forward, but he would not say anything.

'Don't be afraid,' I said. 'It's Carruthers, and – Davies. May we come in, just for a moment?' I gently opened the door wider, while she stepped back and put one hand to her lovely throat. 'Please come downstairs,' I continued. 'We're going to take you and your father to England in the *Dulcibella*, now, at once.'

She had heard me, but her eyes were on Davies. 'I understand not,' she said, with such puzzled sadness that I found it hard to look at her.

'Clara!' said Davies, 'will you not trust us?'

85

I heard a little gasp from her. Suddenly she was in his arms, crying like a tired child, her little white feet between his great clumsy sea-boots, and her rose-brown face on his rough seaman's jacket.

I went downstairs, to find Dollmann putting some papers on the fire. He did not seem to have noticed that the fire was almost out. 'You must be ready in half an hour,' I said, quietly picking up his gun, which lay on the table.

'Take her to England, you two boys. I think I'll stay.'

'Nonsense, she won't go without you.'

Half an hour later, the four of us were hurrying away from the house and down to the harbour. Luckily, Frau Dollmann was away in Hamburg, so there had been no question of her coming with us.

Once on the *Dulcibella*, we hid Clara and her father in the cabin, and sailed straight for the open sea. Nobody seemed to notice our departure. Far away to the south, I thought I saw two dark shapes on the sandbanks. Whether I saw them or not, I knew they were there, and that by the time they were able to move, we would be safe in Holland.

Davies decided to take the route between the islands and the shore, and asked Clara to help him on deck. She was far more useful than I could have been, in my exhausted condition. When I went down to the cabin to fetch the Dutch chart, as we were getting close to the first of the Dutch islands, Dollmann sat up. He seemed in a dream. 'Where are we?' he cried. There was a strange look in his eyes, which I didn't understand at the time, but remembered later.

'Off the coast of Holland,' I replied. I fell asleep soon afterwards, with the yacht rolling and the waves splashing all

Suddenly Clara was in his arms, crying like a tired child.

around me. I did not witness what happened next, since by the time I had heard Davies's cry and climbed up on deck, it was all over. This is his account of the event.

'X came up on deck soon after you went below. He offered to take the helm and show me a short cut, but I knew that one, so I didn't accept his offer. He said nothing, and sat behind us, safe enough, then, to my surprise, he began to talk very sensibly to me about the channel and the buoys and so on. Well, we came to a difficult bit, where I had to concentrate on the helm and the chart, and Clara was busy with the sails, and well – I happened to look round, and he was gone. I think the last thing I heard him say was something about a "short cut" again. He must have slipped over quietly. He had a thick coat and his heavy sea-boots on.'

We sailed about the area for a time, but we never found him.

That evening, we arrived at a small Dutch fishing village on the mainland. We put some fishermen in charge of the yacht, and returned to London by road, rail, and ferry, to lay our information before the government with all possible urgency.

I returned to work at the Foreign Office, where in spite of my best efforts to persuade him, my boss never really believed that I had not received his second letter.

And Davies and Clara? Well, I think I can safely say that Clara has no wish to return to her adopted country, and Davies no longer has any wish to look for adventure on the sands of the North Sea.

A WARNING FOR THE FUTURE

Lying on my writing table, and partly damaged by fire, there is an interesting document. It is a copy of a secret plan for the invasion of England by Germany. Although it is unsigned, it was taken by Carruthers from the fireplace of Dollmann's house at Norderney, so it is quite clear who wrote it. I shall describe what it says, especially for those people who still think Britain is in no danger of being attacked by Germany.

It was an extremely clever plan, based on perfect organization and perfect secrecy. Special barges would be built near seven small coastal harbours, which are hidden from view by the Frisian Islands. At high tide and under cover of darkness, these barges, carrying German soldiers, would be pulled by tugs through the channels between the sandbanks. They would then cross the North Sea and attack the east coast of Britain.

The writer of the document explains the plan in detail. All the work and preparation would be organized by four men (the writer, von Brüning, Böhme, and Grimm), and these four men alone would know the whole plan. Britain would in no way be prepared for such an attack, and the writer is sure that Germany has a good chance of succeeding if the plan is carried out.

I tremble, when I read this document, at what could have happened, if our two adventurers had not discovered the truth in time. I beg you all to be aware of the dangers beyond our shores. Although, for the moment, this particular plan has come to nothing, who knows what might happen in future?

GLOSSARY

account a description of something that has happened, a story

aground (**run/go aground**) if a ship runs/goes aground, it touches the ground in shallow water and cannot move

anchor *(n & v)* a heavy metal object attached to a ship or boat that is dropped into the water to keep the ship in one place

astonish *(v)* to surprise someone very much; **astonishment** *(n)*

barge a large boat with a flat bottom, used on rivers and canals

binoculars special glasses for seeing the details of distant objects

buoy an object that floats on the sea and marks the places where boats can or cannot go

cabin a room on a boat

channel a deep passage of water near a coast that can be used as a route for ships

chart a map of the sea, rivers, etc., used for sailing

colony a country that is governed by people from another, more powerful country

compass an instrument for finding direction, with a needle that always points to the north

crew the people who work on a boat or ship

deck (**on deck**) the floor of a ship

defence the protection of somebody or something from attack

dinghy a small open boat that you sail or row

document written or printed paper with important information

duck *(n)* a common bird that lives on or near water

effort an attempt to do something difficult

embarrassed ashamed; worried about what other people think

faint *(adj)* feeling weak and tired

fiord a long narrow strip of sea between high cliffs

Foreign Office   the British government office in charge of relations with foreign countries

Frau / Fräulein   the German words for 'Mrs' and 'Miss'

gentlemen   a formal way to speak to a group of men

helm   a handle or wheel used for steering a ship

Herr   the German word for 'Mr'

identity   who somebody is

immunity   being protected from trial for a crime

interrupt   to break into a conversation when someone else is talking

invade   to send soldiers into a country to take control of it; **invasion** *(n)*

Kaiser   the title of the German national leader at this time

launch *(n)*   a large motor boat

lead line   a line with a heavy weight at the end, used to measure the depth of water

log-book   the official record of a journey on a ship

loyal   staying faithful to somebody or something

mast   a tall pole on a ship that supports the sails

monument   a building, statue, etc. that reminds people of a famous person or event

navy   the part of a country's armed forces that fights at sea, and the ships that it uses; **naval** *(adj)*

oar   a long pole with a flat blade at one end used to move a boat through the water

on board   on a boat or ship

pilot   a person whose job is to guide ships through a difficult piece of water

publish   to prepare and print a book; **publication** *(n)*

rehearse   to practise something in preparation for the real event in the future; **rehearsal** *(n)*

riddle   a mysterious situation or event that you cannot explain

sandbank   a low hill or raised area of sand in a river or the sea

short cut   a quicker or shorter way of getting to a place

skill   being able to do something well; **skilful** *(adj)*

splash *(n & v)*   the sound when something hits liquid

stepmother   a woman who is married to your father but who is not your real mother

telegram   a short, urgent message sent by electric current along wires, and then printed and delivered

traitor   someone who does something disloyal to his country

trust *(v)*   to have confidence in someone

tug   a small powerful boat for pulling ships

wreck *(n)*   a ship that has sunk or been badly damaged

yacht   a large sailing boat, used for racing or pleasure trips

Before Reading

1 Read the story introduction on the first page of the book, and the back cover. How much do you know now about *The Riddle of the Sands*? For each sentence, circle **Y** (**Yes**) or **N** (**No**).

1 The Frisian Islands are in the Baltic Sea. Y/N
2 Carruthers gets the holiday he expects. Y/N
3 Carruthers agrees to join Davies because he is interested in the mystery. Y/N
4 Arthur Davies enjoys sailing in difficult conditions. Y/N
5 When the two friends start investigating the mystery, the Germans take an interest in them. Y/N
6 When this story was written, relations between Germany and Britain were getting better all the time. Y/N
7 Sailors who like good weather and easy sailing should stay away from the Frisian Islands. Y/N

2 What do you think might happen in the story? Choose from these ideas (as many as you like).

1 One of the friends will . . .
fall in love / turn out to be a spy / get shot / kill someone.
2 Carruthers and Davies will uncover a plot to . . .
kill the British Prime Minister / attack London from the sea / invade Britain.
3 Carruthers and Davies will . . .
capture a spy / wreck a German boat / stop an invasion / warn the British government.

While Reading

Read Chapters 1 to 3, then answer these questions.

1 Why was Carruthers pleased to get Davies' invitation?
2 What made Davies and Carruthers uneasy about each other when they first met?
3 What did Carruthers think of the *Dulcibella* when he first arrived?
4 How did Carruthers' opinion of Davies change?
5 What mystery did Carruthers discover when he looked in the *Dulcibella's* logbook?
6 What reasons did Carruthers give for not wanting to go to the North Sea?
7 What worries did Bartels have about Davies?
8 Why did Davies get into difficulties when he reached the Telte channel?
9 How did Davies know that Dollmann was English?
10 Why was the coast from Borkum to the Elbe so important to Germany?

Before you read Chapter 4, can you guess the answer to this question?

What warning will Commander von Brüning give the friends when they meet?
1 To leave the Frisian Islands   3 To be careful of local people
2 To stay away from Dollmann   4 To be careful of thick fog

Read Chapters 4 to 6. Who said these words, and to whom? Who or what were they talking about?

1 'It's a pity you missed her.'
2 'The only way to understand a place like this is to explore it at low tide.'
3 'They're all seamen and know how important it is.'
4 'We must be very careful what we say to him.'
5 'He couldn't have seen what happened. Anyway, it didn't matter.'
6 'He has the most terrifying adventures, and makes them sound perfectly ordinary.'
7 'Everyone on these islands knows all about it.'
8 'You know how your friend feels. I wouldn't encourage him, if I were you.'
9 'I find it very difficult to talk about things like this.'
10 'There are no clues to be got from her.'
11 'I know he'll be very sorry, but you can always trust him to do the right thing.'
12 'Perhaps he thought I'd recognized him. That explains everything!'

Before you read Chapter 7, can you guess what happens next? Choose some of these ideas.

1 Carruthers and Davies row to Memmert in the fog.
2 Carruthers and Davies meet Dollmann in Norderney town.
3 Davies receives a letter from Clara.
4 Von Brüning tries to arrest Carruthers and Davies as spies.
5 Carruthers and Davies are invited to dinner at Dollmann's house the next evening.

Read Chapters 7 to 9, and complete Carruthers' account of his adventures with the names of people and places given below. Some names will be needed more than once.

Amsterdam	*London*	*Clara*	*von Brüning*	*Grimm*
Bensersiel	*Memmert*	*Davies*	*Dollmann*	*the Kaiser*
Esens	*Norderney*	*Böhme*	*Frau Dollmann*	

Outside the office on _____, I listened to the four men discussing a report. After _____ and _____ left, _____ and _____ then talked secretly about a plan for the 25th. Later, _____ and I rowed back to the *Dulcibella*, where we found _____, _____, and _____ on board, looking at our things. We had dinner with them that night at _____'s house; _____ and _____ were also there.

Next day I left _____ with _____ and travelled to _____, where I sent a telegram to _____. Then I went by train to _____, and saw barges being built. On the night of the 25th I went to _____, and hid on a tug. _____ was steering, and _____ and _____ were there too, with a third man, whom I recognized as _____. When I realized the trip was a rehearsal for an invasion, I took a risk. I pretended to be _____, took the helm, and steered the tug into a sandbank. In the confusion I took the tug's dinghy, rowed to _____, and rejoined _____ on the *Dulcibella*.

What will happen in Chapter 10? Choose some of these ideas.

1 Dollmann refuses to leave / agrees to leave / is taken back to England by force / never reaches England / shoots Davies.

2 Clara stays in Norderney / leaves with Carruthers and Davies / goes back to England / never speaks to Davies again.

3 Davies is injured in a fight with Dollmann / takes Clara to England / lets Dollmann go for Clara's sake.

After Reading

1 **Perhaps this is what some of the characters in the story were thinking. Which characters are they, and what is about to happen in the story at this moment?**

1 'Still no answer. That's good – they must both have gone to the town. Now, better put that mast light out first. Then I'll go down into the cabin and start having a look round in there . . .'

2 'I'm so glad he came back. After that awful weather the day we sailed to Cuxhaven I thought I'd never see him again. I do like this dear little cabin. So untidy! And all those books! That one looks . . . Oh no, oh no!'

3 'Some holiday this is going to be – a miserable little boat, nobody to do the work, hardly enough room down there to stand up. I think I'll go outside – at least it's not raining.'

4 'It's lucky I'm the same size as Grimm. That sailor didn't suspect anything, I'm sure of it. Just a little bit further, I think, then I'll make my move. Increase the speed . . . and . . . now!'

5 'It's all over now, I suppose. Better try and burn as many of these papers as I can. They'll be downstairs again in a minute. I wish they'd just take her and go. But I know she won't leave unless I do . . . so I'll have to go with them . . .'

6 'They might be quite harmless. Just here for the duck-shooting. But I wonder . . . And I don't like the sound of this Dollmann business. I think I'll have a quiet word in the friend's ear . . .'

2 Complete this conversation between von Brüning and Dollmann
   about the attempt to kill Davies. Use as many words as you like.

VON BRÜNING: Well, Herr Dollmann, I had a most interesting
   conversation in Bensersiel the other day with a friend of yours.

DOLLMANN: _____

VON BRÜNING: Herr Davies – the young Englishman from the
   Dulcibella. You look surprised, Dollmann.

DOLLMANN: _____

VON BRÜNING: I don't think you were expecting to see him ever
   again! In fact, wasn't that your plan?

DOLLMANN: _____

VON BRÜNING: So you left him to be smashed to pieces on the
   Hohenhörn? You fool! Don't you see how bad it looks?

DOLLMANN: _____

VON BRÜNING: But he's still exploring round the islands – and
   now he's got a friend with him, a friend from the *Foreign
   Office*! That's a real worry. What are they up to?

DOLLMANN: _____

VON BRÜNING: Herr Dollmann, the last thing in the world I
   intend to do is leave you to deal with these Englishmen by
   yourself. From now on, you don't go near them without me.

3 At dinner at the Dollmanns' house, people are saying one thing and
   almost certainly thinking another. What do you think the
   characters are *really* thinking as they say these words?

   1 Böhme: 'I'm going to Bremen, so we'll travel as far as Leer
      together. How pleasant!'
   2 Von Brüning: 'I'm not very closely involved in all this. Try the
      company director. Rescue me, Herr Dollmann!'

3 Von Brüning: 'I thought I was being most helpful to you, giving advice about duck shooting and so on.'

4 Dollmann: 'Come, let's hear it. Your wild ideas are amusing.'

5 Carruthers: 'We were a little surprised to find you all on board the *Dulcibella*, taking such a deep interest in a small boat. I think you wanted to *inspect* us!'

6 Dollmann: 'Gentlemen, we must come to an agreement with this dangerous young man. What can we offer Herr Carruthers?'

7 Carruthers: 'Ah, you don't read English easily, perhaps. I expect Herr Böhme does.'

4 **What are your opinions on the characters and ideas in the story? Discuss these questions.**

1 The story does not tell us why Dollmann decided to jump off the *Dulcibella*. How many possible reasons can you think of to explain his decision?

2 The story does not tell us if Clara knew about her father's spying activities. If she had known he was a traitor, should she have done something about it? Or is duty to your family more important than duty to your country?

3 Was Dollmann right to jump, in your opinion? Or should he have gone back to England to be tried in the law courts as a traitor? Were Davies and Carruthers to blame for not ensuring that Dollmann stayed alive to face his trial?

4 Has spying always existed as an activity, in any society? Is it acceptable to spy for your own country, against another country? Is it less acceptable to spy for *another* country, against your *own* country?

5 *The Riddle of the Sands* is said to be the first great modern spy story. How have spy stories changed since 1903?

5 **Here is Davies, thinking about the holiday that he and Carruthers are going to have. Choose the best words (one for each gap) to complete his thoughts.**

Oh dear! Perhaps inviting Carruthers wasn't _____ a good idea after all. He _____ to have a huge amount of _____ with him. How on earth are _____ going to get that big case _____ the *Dulcibella*? And what kind of _____ is he expecting? I wish I _____ given this more thought before I _____ to him. After all, we don't _____ know each other very well. What _____ we can't stand each other? A _____ yacht is no place to be _____ somebody you dislike.

Then there's the _____ with Dollmann. What should I tell _____ about that? Perhaps I should come _____ with it straight away – but no, _____ to wait until he's got used _____ things. I suppose I could try _____ persuade him to come to the _____ Islands first, and then see what _____ when we get there. But I _____ want to have to lie to _____ – if there's one thing I'm not _____ at, it's lying, and I'll just _____ everything worse. Well, it's too late _____ second thoughts now, I suppose – he's _____ .

6 **Here are some new titles for the ten chapters of *The Riddle of the Sands*. Decide which title goes with which chapter, and write the chapter number next to the title.**

___ Exploring the sands   ___ Talking to the commander

___ Listening at a window   ___ First signs of a mystery

___ A letter from Germany   ___ Carruthers goes exploring

___ Passengers for England   ___ Dining with danger

___ A visit from Clara   ___ The tale of a dangerous voyage

ABOUT THE AUTHOR

Robert Erskine Childers was born in 1870 in London. He grew up in Ireland, studied at Cambridge, and from 1895 to 1910 he worked as a clerk at the House of Commons. During his holidays he enjoyed sailing along the coastlines of Holland, Denmark, and Germany. He fought in the South African War of 1899–1902, and published his only novel, *The Riddle of the Sands*, in 1903. In the same year he met and married an American, Mollie Osgood, and the couple often sailed their fifty-foot yacht *Asgard* in the North Sea and the Baltic.

In 1910 he took up the cause of Irish independence, and wrote a book on the subject the following year. He and his wife used *Asgard* to smuggle guns and ammunition into Ireland in 1914 for the Irish rebels. During the First World War he did reconnaissance and intelligence work for the British Navy, and after the war ended he settled in Ireland, became a member of Sinn Féin, and was elected to the Irish Parliament. In the Irish civil war he joined the republican army, and was captured and executed by a firing squad in 1922. His son, Erskine Hamilton Childers, was President of Ireland from 1973 to 1974.

John Buchan said of him: 'No revolution ever produced a nobler or purer spirit', but Winston Churchill disagreed: 'No man has done more harm or done more genuine malice or endeavoured to bring a greater curse upon the common people of Ireland than this strange being, actuated by a deadly and malignant hatred for the land of his birth'.

However, most people agree that *The Riddle of the Sands* has a place in literature as one of the first great spy stories.

OXFORD BOOKWORMS LIBRARY

Classics • Crime & Mystery • Factfiles • Fantasy & Horror
Human Interest • Playscripts • Thriller & Adventure
True Stories • World Stories

The OXFORD BOOKWORMS LIBRARY provides enjoyable reading in English, with a wide range of classic and modern fiction, non-fiction, and plays. It includes original and adapted texts in seven carefully graded language stages, which take learners from beginner to advanced level. An overview is given on the next pages.

All Stage 1 titles are available as audio recordings, as well as over eighty other titles from Starter to Stage 6. All Starters and many titles at Stages 1 to 4 are specially recommended for younger learners. Every Bookworm is illustrated, and Starters and Factfiles have full-colour illustrations.

The OXFORD BOOKWORMS LIBRARY also offers extensive support. Each book contains an introduction to the story, notes about the author, a glossary, and activities. Additional resources include tests and worksheets, and answers for these and for the activities in the books. There is advice on running a class library, using audio recordings, and the many ways of using Oxford Bookworms in reading programmes. Resource materials are available on the website <www.oup.com/bookworms>.

The *Oxford Bookworms Collection* is a series for advanced learners. It consists of volumes of short stories by well-known authors, both classic and modern. Texts are not abridged or adapted in any way, but carefully selected to be accessible to the advanced student.

You can find details and a full list of titles in the *Oxford Bookworms Library Catalogue* and *Oxford English Language Teaching Catalogues*, and on the website <www.oup.com/bookworms>.

THE OXFORD BOOKWORMS LIBRARY
GRADING AND SAMPLE EXTRACTS

STARTER • 250 HEADWORDS

present simple – present continuous – imperative –
can/cannot, must – *going to* (future) – simple gerunds ...

Her phone is ringing – but where is it?

Sally gets out of bed and looks in her bag. No phone. She looks under the bed. No phone. Then she looks behind the door. There is her phone. Sally picks up her phone and answers it. *Sally's Phone*

STAGE 1 • 400 HEADWORDS

... past simple – coordination with *and*, *but*, *or* –
subordination with *before*, *after*, *when*, *because*, *so* ...

I knew him in Persia. He was a famous builder and I worked with him there. For a time I was his friend, but not for long. When he came to Paris, I came after him – I wanted to watch him. He was a very clever, very dangerous man. *The Phantom of the Opera*

STAGE 2 • 700 HEADWORDS

... present perfect – *will* (future) – *(don't) have to, must not, could* –
comparison of adjectives – simple *if* clauses – past continuous –
tag questions – *ask/tell* + infinitive ...

While I was writing these words in my diary, I decided what to do. I must try to escape. I shall try to get down the wall outside. The window is high above the ground, but I have to try. I shall take some of the gold with me – if I escape, perhaps it will be helpful later. *Dracula*

... should, may – present perfect continuous – *used to* – past perfect –
causative – relative clauses – indirect statements ...

Of course, it was most important that no one should see Colin, Mary, or Dickon entering the secret garden. So Colin gave orders to the gardeners that they must all keep away from that part of the garden in future. ***The Secret Garden***

STAGE 4 • 1400 HEADWORDS

... past perfect continuous – passive (simple forms) –
would conditional clauses – indirect questions –
relatives with *where/when* – gerunds after prepositions/phrases ...

I was glad. Now Hyde could not show his face to the world again. If he did, every honest man in London would be proud to report him to the police. ***Dr Jekyll and Mr Hyde***

STAGE 5 • 1800 HEADWORDS

... future continuous – future perfect –
passive (modals, continuous forms) –
would have conditional clauses – modals + perfect infinitive ...

If he had spoken Estella's name, I would have hit him. I was so angry with him, and so depressed about my future, that I could not eat the breakfast. Instead I went straight to the old house. ***Great Expectations***

STAGE 6 • 2500 HEADWORDS

... passive (infinitives, gerunds) – advanced modal meanings –
clauses of concession, condition

When I stepped up to the piano, I was confident. It was as if I knew that the prodigy side of me really did exist. And when I started to play, I was so caught up in how lovely I looked that I didn't worry how I would sound. ***The Joy Luck Club***